Cardboard Spaceship

Jean-Paul L. Garnier

Dedicated to Eric Fomley, champion of short form science fiction. And to all of the small presses out there keeping literature fresh and alive.

Contents

Introduction

Reading the digital MS of *Carboard Spaceship* I had a déjà vu feeling. There was a maddening uncertainty about where and when. Some of the pieces I had read in periodicals, but most were new and the whole had elements of textual collage. It took a while to realise the experience was throwing me back to a different time when I was a lot younger, which began as a seventeen-year-old waiting impatiently for the next monthly copy of *New Worlds* to drop on my doormat. The stories in *Cardboard Spaceship* have the same keen urgency.

I had come across the work of Jean Paul L Garnier before in a 2020 novella published at the height of the Covid pandemic. 'This book is dedicated to 'Corporate America and its attitude to short term gain in exchange for long term tragedy', it states decisively at the front of *Garbage In, Gospel Out*, before describing a world very like our own. It follows the life of everyman Frank, a fantasist with problems at home who suffers from ADHD and has allowed himself to be corralled as a jobbing journalist for the sinister Bureau. The make-believe future this unholy alliance helps to produce seems to typify the populist world of conspiracy theory and gangsterism into which the real twenty-first century is descending, in which a family that is a cross between *Dallas* and *The Beverley Hillbillies* rules and where runaway technology has been allowed to enable a new and virtual reality. It is a world in which anything goes – until it doesn't. 'Incorrect or poor-quality input will always produce faulty output', is a sub-heading from the same book.

To replicate Frank's talent for fake news Garnier utilises the fold-in technique of cut-up writing used in the 1950's, employed, ironically, by its co-inventor Williams Burroughs as a means of breaking down reality that he held is being spun on us by *real* alien invaders. Frank finds his subversive talent is greatly favoured by the anonymous Bureau officials, and it is used to conjure the scenario of a myth of a near future that leaks backward to consume everything.

In recent research, ADHD is thought to be a left-over trait from humanity's hunter-gathering stage of development, where 'unrestrained flightiness with an obsessive fixation' (a line from *Garbage In, Gospel Out*) is a survival advantage; more can be harvested by moving rapidly from patch to patch than harvesting one patch to exhaustion before moving on. The condition has lost its value – except perhaps by a denizen of the head-scrambling science fictional world of today; and I feel that's the point that's being made. Some of the pieces, that make up *Cardboard Spaceship*, like the opening 'The Names of My Children', in which a man is abducted by his mistress and taken through a burning landscape away from his wife and family, are about the wild present or the even wilder near-future, characterised by an imaginative precocity and painted with an impressionistic intensity that has the effect of humanising writing in an age where values are being replaced by machine production and dissipated by social media.

One of the reasons for the emergence of a 'new wave' of Science Fiction in the 1960's was because the pace of technology was increasing at such a rate that spaceflight and the colonisation of other worlds seemed within reach; the future appeared to have collapsed, and what was happening now, in an underexplored and ever-burgeoning present, began to exercise the imaginations of some of the writers of that time. When reworking one of his 'speculative fiction' novels for republication by a demanding new publisher, Charles Platt wrote to me in 1975 that, as he sat down to think how to approach the update, it seemed to him that society was – and I quote from his letter – "accelerating on a roller coaster to self-destruction [when] it's going to be like living in a dozen different end-of-the-world science fiction scenarios... I'm trying to anticipate the scenes... but it's all happening so fast that I can't keep up. History is more than ever likely to outdate whatever I write, almost before I finish writing it." Platt wrote this almost fifty years ago, and it seemed even then to herald an unstable time in which there might be no future, in keeping with the views of Ballard, Toffler and others. By then, *New Worlds* had passed its best years, but it had done its work.

Garbage In, Gospel Out seemed to anticipate this omnipresent increasingly violent 'now' as much as the best prophetic work being produced in the unfolding penumbra cast by the sixties – by Michael Moorcock, JG Ballard, Alan Moore, William Gibson, William Burroughs – and the variety and breadth of Garnier's new stories reflect this eternal present, perhaps an end-world, and with *Cardboard Spaceship* seems to be Garnier's starting premise. His stories are compelling examples of this truth-telling and display an astonishing breadth of invention – the cry of an author who feels the need to vocalise very real fears as a means both to free himself of what he knows and to warn others.

Many of these pieces are unified by a first-person voice. It is the authentic voice of NOW even if his topic is – and it sometimes is – a more traditional science fiction story. Stories of psychological horror, vignettes of absurdity, slight but intensely poetic narratives sit alongside science fiction, and the book – speculative in the original meaning of speculative fiction; of now, or of the near-future – is the better for it.

Many pieces turn on personal experience and observation. The Bradburyesque 'The Day the Hooks Came', about an epidemic of abductions as people are irresistibly attracted by gifts representing their dreams and are whisked away, is based on the author's remembrances of small-town America sadly now mostly gone. In 'Night Patrol' a six-year-old, garbed as a Ninja, watches over his home as he protects his family; a fantasy rooted in many childhoods. Observation of calamity often turns to biting satire. 'Western Expansion', a portentous fantasy premised on the author's own Mojave Desert in California, conjures a personified desert, alive and mocking, as it spreads across the globe, and 'Over Night' features the first election of an American president by lottery. 'An Off the Record Letter', about what *really* goes on amongst the astronauts and cosmonauts inside their capsules, is a tale as far away from American values as you can get. In this category probably also comes 'Homo Paniscus', a grisly black comedy reminiscent of Poe about animal experimentation when a group of university academics attempt to prove whether we are the products of evolution or creation. Other stories, such as 'Free Download', are by turns amusing, but one in particular, 'Blue Gemini One', is extremely scary; you can imagine it as an episode in a tense film. Bracketed with this, 'Disophonia' (a play on 'misophonia'), describes how a lone passenger aboard a star ship tormented by the silence, gives up and joins the void outside. In 'We Are Not Safe Here', a tribute to Philip K Dick, the characters in a novel locked away in a safe for protection come alive and blast their way out. In 'Electrosmooth', a hirsute boy teased at school finds a novel solution to unwanted hair.

Two of the most powerful pieces in this collection are 'Fucking Like Animals', where clubbers – in convincing dance scenes – take the animal hormones 'Bird', 'Cat' and 'Rat', with unforeseen consequences, and the final 'Birth of Fire', about the emotions of love and loss produced by desperately partial cheating partners contrasted with the impartial melee of universal processes. It has some of the most accomplished poetic passages in the book, and both stories display another sub-theme running throughout: relationships.

These twenty-one brief stories also reminded of the pleasures of other youthful reading, such as *Tomato Cain*, screenwriter Nigel Kneale's 1949 collection of short stories, which drew me in with their novel, hard-boiled storytelling. Kneale's publisher wanted a novel, but Kneale didn't, and gave him *Tomato Cain* instead. I slipped just as easily into Garnier's poetic sometimes impressionistic narratives of the near future as I did into those tales written at the beginning of the increasingly unstable 20th century; when it seemed like society was engulfed in endless war. And here another thought occurs. The day of big novels may be coming to an end, and short storytelling might be having a long overdue come-back. Let's hope.

Michael Butterworth
4 Sandino Court
April 2024

The Names of My Children

The vehicle made it clear that passengers would take a back seat. It moved through the cool, wet city taking us further from the safe zone. Leanna gazed down her long nose at me, her face in the half-light became more severe than usual. She tapped a code with her forefinger into the glowing dash. It was my car but it only wanted her touch. Somewhere back in the fire surrounded mists my family waited, trusting that I would return to the shelter. The air crackled with electricity killing my hope that we would be going back any time soon.

Emergency situations like that suck firefighters within the area. In undulating waves they came to help, only to find that the available hardware wanted someone to play with. The solar radiation, the adult babies and red flag warnings had not been enough. My vehicle, which was not Leanna's, curved through the burning spaces propelling us toward the great concrete bunkers. Research into adaptive events had killed at least thirteen people so far. The numbers would no doubt rise. But Leanna continued to smile as though a plan of hers was working out nicely. My family would disagree.

"You always fail me. Your car isn't much better. Can't you see how the flames lick at the heavens? The city is yours, too bad there will be little left in the end. I could be yours but you cower under that suit of yours. Even the firemen have learned that the signal enters through the skin. Damn civilians. Ate it up just like the commercials told you to. You know they are testing you, yet here you are with me, infinitely wiser than you. Keeping you safe even as we flee your dreams."

Leanna, condescending as always. Took from me as she pleased. Sirens pierced through the smoke. A hundred houses burned all along what were once my streets. My suit tightened further. Skin crawled with anticipation knowing the harm and wanting it badly. Leanna looked towards me smiling, teeth glowing orange. She matched the sky in most regards but she wasn't falling for it. She navigated the flames as though they were imaginary. Perhaps they were but I could still hear screams matching the volume of the moving sirens.

From the window I saw a man tearing at his suit. The buckles changed position as he clawed at them. The colors changed until he could not tell his own body from the surrounding wreckage. His fingers bled as he tried to remove the asphalt from the burning road circling his feet. Comical dances completed the horror music that dragged through the suburban night. Police fired warning shots straight up. Pop, pop, pop. They were trying to time the shots with the rest of the music. The dancing man falls to ashes. Leanna's smile grows in intensity. They flash from orange into rainbows or terror, but it is not her terror, she is feeding on the ruptured waves of the satellite. She didn't need a suit, her mind had undone the frequencies prior to my abduction.

As when old men throw yet another log onto the fire the sparks spiral into the whirling void. The fire sings like an out of tune children's choir. The parents sit with pleased looks on their faces as they endure the cacophony. My children have become tinder by now. Leanna sings a poisonous lullaby with touches of triumph. She believes she has freed me from the shackles of modernity. While it isn't true I am elated by the ever tightening suit. They knew to make our downfall entertaining but who knew it could be this rapturous. I squirmed in my seat to the rhythm of the screams. Pop, scream, pop, pop, scream. Leanna writhed in gross pleasure knowing I couldn't hold out much longer.

Sun falls behind a new tower of smoke. The debris starts assembling into the wall we must pass. The car coos at her touch. She reaches out to it like an animal in heat. The controls are warm by the fire which employs all directions. Firemen spray each other with hoses, ignoring the blaze. A racing pack of dogs leaps from their last meal into the burning windows of what had once been my office. The same room where the code was identified and my life was brought to its knees. Gazing into muddy knee prints, the faces of my children stare back, expressionless.

I don't need the skin transmission to know what comes next. I caved to her along the way, she stopped smiling at the moment of connection. She enjoys the game more than victory. When I tear up she slaps me and the vehicle skids to a halt in the embers. Her eyes say "get out". Fear has paralyzed me but the fire awaits. The suit reinforces her decision. Trying to mouth the names of my children I fall from the open door. Leanna slams it behind me and stares through the window. My suit becomes yellow. Hungry flames counter the change by turning blue. All of the city lit up like neon. The burning blue eats families. Tasting my wife's disappointment I join the fire in its pursuit.

The firemen spray me down, all the while chanting in playground sing-song. Leanna dances on the roof of the car she has purchased from me with pain. The suit turns the same blue as the growing torrent. I can't tell my body from the fire now. Sweat stings my eyes that sparkle in all Leanna's dancing glory. I know now that I wanted defeat. Still singing, the firemen turn off the water and reconnect the hoses to an over-turned gasoline truck. The signals from the satellite become visible through the billowing black smoke. I tear at my suit only to find it has become one with my flesh. Leanna zeros in on me, sensing the joining. Her smile is cobalt blue now. She is tonguing a tooth, looking for the source of the signal. She kneels on the roof and bangs her face into the warming metal. Spits the tooth at me. It crawls into the suit pocket and strengthens the satellite's outpour. It's all clear to me now.

Everything smells of gasoline as they cleanse our modern achievements. Again they wet me down. The wavelengths are visible to us alone. Pulling the tooth from the pocket my suit resists. Managing to wiggle it free I swallow it and find the signal strengthening still. Blue light emits from my mouth. I forget the names of my children, trying to call out for them but only repeating Leanna's name. She mocks the mannerisms of my wife and I know then that Leanna is all that remains of the people I once knew. She knows it too. She basks in her success. The suit is overtaking me. "Crawl toward the flames" loops in what's left of my mind, nearly replaced by the satellite.

"You lack what the fire wants." She scolds me even as I am engulfed. She sneers that I don't belong where the family ended up. "Drag that hollow suit to the office" she commands. I am putty to her. Again the signal comes on strong. She's an antenna for my fears. My skin makes the crinkling sounds of pork rinds munched by the devil. The sound joins the signal and enters the cosmos piggybacked on the microwave carrier. A blue streak X's out my periphery. She has left along with the car. I can't tell her laughter from the flames. The faces of my family wash away down the steaming gutter. Firemen are clearing the slag from the streets. I flow with the mess. In a river of Leanna's tears I dream of repeating the last days. Her tooth is the last thing I can know. Words gone. Suit tightens further. Signal dissolves the last flesh with luminous intensity. My name puffs into smoke along with the others.

The Day the Hooks Came

I t didn't seem strange because we had all heard of the space elevator. None of us had seen one but we knew it was some kind of cable from the sky. Why they wanted to make something like that, we couldn't say. Guess they weren't happy here on Earth. Some wanted to leave, others just wanted to go back to the simple life. The world moved so fast in those days that most folks stopped trying to keep up at all. A lot of things had simply grown too complicated for the average Joe to comprehend, so they became invisible in plain sight.

I was walking down Main Street the first time I saw one. On my way to the diner for lunch as usual. I met Betty there at noon three times a week. It was our ritual. Everyone always thought we were a couple, or suggested that we become one, but it wasn't like that. I smiled at her through the window. She was sitting in our usual booth, a cup of coffee already waiting for me. As I rounded the corner heading for the door, I saw it. Looked like a piece of aircraft cable but smooth, hanging right out of the sky like it belonged there. A man almost walked straight into it and stumbled back. A crowd started to gather.

"Are you sure you should be touching that?" I called out to the brave kid that was slowly advancing on the object and poking at it with a stick. He ran off without answering.

A few of the pedestrians shrugged and walked away, already bored of the object. It wasn't that unusual for some new-fangled tech thingy to be hooked up to the lampposts or what not. Things were always changing, so we stopped seeing the changes. Most folks had turned their curiosity inward, if anywhere. I too lost interest and didn't want to keep Betty waiting any longer.

"Get lost on your way in?" she teased.

"Just chasing off the street urchins. Some new piece of tech hanging out of the sky. Never can tell if it's supposed to be there or if some kid is going to get hurt." I said over the rim of the coffee. It smelled good, and she had put exactly the right amount of cream in for my taste.

We chatted about our days and ordered sandwiches. In the corner of my eye I could see Steve, the cook, shaking his head. He always did this when he saw us, as if to say, "what a waste, you obviously love each other." And we did, just not in that way.

The screech of brakes drew my attention from the counter. Betty gasped. Outside the window a commotion was breaking out. A car had almost hit some of the kids hanging out on the curb. People were shouting too, but not at the driver. He got out of his car and joined the gaping crowd, all pointing up and exclaiming in hushed voices.

"What do you figure they're getting on about?" Betty asked.

I was about to tell her that I didn't know when a man broke off from the crowd and came into the diner shouting, "It took Jimmy! He's gone. Went straight up into the sky." He was in a kind of panic and spoke to try and figure out what's real, more so than to inform anyone.

"Well, that was more exciting than most lunches." Betty said sarcastically while looking at her watch. We finished our sandwiches and went Dutch on the bill. As usual I was going to walk her back to work. Outside there was still a crowd. Some of them pointed up and a few were shouting.

One man wagged his finger disapprovingly. "I tell you I saw it first. He had no right to cut me off, it was mine fair and square." There was genuine anger in his voice.

"Hold on for a second, Betty." I approached the man slowly, curious what all the hubbub was about. "Excuse me, sir. What did you see first? What's going on here?"

He looked at me, eyes filled with fresh anger. "That cable that came down from the sky, that was for me. Had a check with my name on it. I saw the figure too. It was exactly the sum I needed to save my business. A gift from heaven if you ask me. And then that guy ran up, saying something about dreams of flying, grabbed the cable, and went sailing up into the sky. Took the check with him too. I tell you it isn't right, it was meant for me."

I heard what he said but it wasn't making a lot of sense to me. Betty was tugging on my sleeve, so I turned, forgetting all about the man and his "check from heaven".

Crowds were gathered all over the sidewalk on both sides of the street. Some were arguing and then a gasp overtook the crowds as another pedestrian shot up into the sky holding onto another of the cables for dear life.

I took Betty by the hand. "Those cables are everywhere. What do you think is going on?" I could feel Betty's hand go all clammy. She squeezed tighter out of fear.

"I don't know, Frank. Folks are acting pretty strange. I don't like it." she replied.

We headed north in the direction of Betty's office, fortunately away from the growing throng. Betty loosened her grip on my hand, slowly calming down. But the commotion behind us continued. We made it two blocks up the road without incident. Then across the street another cable dropped through the clear blue sky down to the sidewalk. A man ran up to it exclaiming nothing but joy.

"All my dreams come true! I can't believe it. I've waited my whole life for something..."

I couldn't hear the rest of what he said as he was yanked up into the air and out of earshot. Betty's nails dug into my hand. "Oh, Frank. What's going on?"

I didn't have an answer for her but when I looked around I saw cables coming down all over the block. Running people headed toward them, some of them fighting to get there first. And all of them were exuberant. Smiles painted with tears, many shouting, faces looking like prayers were being answered in real time. And the cables took them one by one. The street was growing emptier by the minute.

Another cable fell right in front of us. The rest of the street blurred to nothing as the cable came into focus. Sparkling in front of me was a ring in a little ornate box. The same I had eyed for years in the jeweler's window. The one I let myself think about and get carried away dreaming of a life with Betty that we both knew was not meant to be. I reached out for it and Betty quickly slapped my hand away.

"That's mine!" she snapped.

How did she know? I had never admitted it to anyone, not even fully to myself. But the anger in her eyes was real. She looked at me as though I was trying to steal her most prized possession. It didn't make sense, she never got angry with me.

"What do you mean, Betty? What do you see?" I tried to keep my voice calm. She reached for the cable and I stalled her hand. "Betty, tell me what you're seeing."

She looked entranced. All the crowds did. She reached again and this time I had to use some force to prevent her from grabbing the cable. It only served to make her madder.

"All my life I've had one big unattainable dream," she started, "and now it's here in front of me and you're trying to stop me from having it."

"I'm not following you. What do you mean? What do you see?"

Now there were tears in her eyes. "Can't you see it too? It's a plane ticket with my name on it. My prayers are answered, I finally get to go to Paris."

"Betty, I don't think it's real. That's not what I see. I see the ring that I always wanted to get for you..." Now I'd done it. I'd admitted what I had promised myself I would never admit. There was no going back, now she knew.

"No! It's a plane ticket!" She pushed me out of the way and latched onto the cable. In seconds her feet were above my head and I reached out to try and grab her but only came away with a single shoe. She was gone, and with her my private dream.

The streets were almost empty now and it had grown quiet. Cables still hung down from the sky but the few of us left did not reach for them. Wonderment filled the faces of the people who hadn't been taken. Tears were abundant. Some of them had the look of deep loss. I thought about my father taking me fishing all those years ago. He had told me his secret on that father son trip.

"The trick to catching a fish, son, is to have the right bait for the right fish. If you show'um something that looks just like what they want they'll jump right onto your hook and practically beg for the frying pan."

Phrogger

Through a crack in the plaster I watched him jack in. Tell-tale twitch of the legs as juice surged through the plug in the neck into the body. Probably two hours of free reign. If, that is, this was part of the daily routine and not just a random stop in for a quick shop, or spank, or whatever he does in there.

I made my way through the crawl space and into the kitchen. Have to eat while you can. I heard him stir and froze. Was it a short one this time? No, just another kick. He must be getting a good jolt in there. Yep, it'll be a hour at least. Looking in two directions I keep an eye on him in the living room, smear peanut butter on toast. The look on his face when he finds the empty jar is priceless every time. Keep it coming boy.

Food ate, I move into the living room, sit next to him. I need to jack in too, it'll have to wait til he sleeps. Last time I went in too, almost forgot to get out before him. Got lost in Krissy's dive. Easy to do in that shit pit of vipers and pleasure. Krissy had me all juiced up, blanking hard – eyes all white. Would have spaced too and stayed past my welcome – saw him come in and bounced in a hurry, still Fogged up – but just in time to not have to face him. I'd be like a mirror of ugly – scent all familiar but no face he could place. A ghost riding him somewhere in the back of his head – an artifact of the cable jacking him. So he'd think anyway. Fled quick too. Got out in time to see him twitch from the Fog.

But he never guested he had a Phrogger. But here I am looking for the milk, all lip smack and smug. Waiting for my turn on the inside. I'd worried he followed me to Krissy's, but how could that be?

Gotta tell Krissy to watch out for him. If he echoes I'm fucked. We're close enough as it is. Can't get too close – if he echoes and we merge – can't go there – I'll be toast. Maybe I gotta find a new place to Fog up. Old favs always dying on me. Phrogger life, you know.

Been thinkin on this too long. Back to the wall before he turns. I do love the moments of mobility – not as good as the inside but he does have PB, for now at least. Consider taking the jar with me but he might forget to get more if it isn't in his face. Reminder of jacked forgetfulness. Hangover's the only thing that returns with you. Especially if you've been at Krissy's. One more spoon and I'm back at the crack watching out at him looking for the signs of return. He's all sweat and quiet. Don't know where else he goes but judging by the beads on his face he likes heavy. One of these days he'll stay in, stop with the rent – on the streets I'll be looking for a new mark. Always takes too long. Fog starts liftin and I'm in trouble.

Here he comes. Got back in the wall just in time, again. Have to suppress a fit of coughing when I see him. It's been too long since I was in. Sleep you MF. He won't though. It'll be hours yet. He heads to the PB, priceless look as he spins the lid back to the almost empty jar. Stands blank in front of the fridge, all sweats, tryin to cool off. Sleep, buddy. That'll work. But he doesn't. Goes to the living room again and eyes the jack. Oh come on – my turn already.

Knows it's a bad idea and he still does it. Surge is quieter this time as he jacks. No twitch – Fog's got him. Fine you shit the PB's mine. Gotta stave off he ache somehow. I could sleep standing up if I gotta stay in the wall too long. If he gets stuck on the ride it's gonna be a long night for me. I join him in the sweats. I could creep out again but maybe he's just in for another sweet taste. If he sleeps on me I'm fucked. What a waste of in-time. Brother you don't know how good you've got it. Your Phrogger shadow can't hold out forever.

Hours later I'm moving past urgent. He's sleeping on me. Hands all dangling not bothering to wipe anymore. Out as can be. Gonna have to risk the echo if it goes on.

Hours pass. Fuck it I'm jacking in. He's still on the couch. Sweat dripping. He must have found a good place. I'd follow if it weren't for the echo risk. Must be a good one though. Typically he drops out. Two hour max.

Jitters are comin. I could roll him like a sleeping dog. Gotta remember who's frontin the bill. Hard to care at this point. If it's Fog someone's got a new batch. Can almost smell it comin off him. Worth the risk? If he's on one like I think he won't be keeping this place for long. Moving anyway... Probably worth it. No place to jack though. Jitter gets in charge. See ya judgment.

Sitting down next to him again almost like the dreaded echo. Hard to care this far out of the inside. Little spasm knocks me back to the room. He's quivering good. Looks good too. Auxiliary jack in hand. Pause but the decision is on me Fog looks to good. In. Down to Krissy's. Hollers inform me the night's goin. Juicers all over. Music thump. I Fog up, Krissy's drippin in the good stuff. Clouds come on all sweet and right. My usual hours but never sittin right next to him all couched up and oblivious. Thick Fog. Definitely a new batch. Music morphs into muscle at this stage. Flow you fucker. Easy to forget the out world.

He walks in. Hard to believe he's walkin. Even with the sweat. Must juice hard as me. Wouldn't know in the domestic. Fucker walks steady too. Lookin at Krissy she's got no advice. Wouldn't know anyway. He's all mirror and fear. For me at least. Fog's thick killing all care.

Nod takes the time. I drip back to Krissy's. He sittin at my table, hard stare, sweat all beading. "I know you?" voice all syrupy smooth.

"Nope." trying not to see. Fog's got me locked into the chair as the echo starts chiming – in the bad way. Mouth might as well be all peanut buttered out. Real world spilling. It gets bad. Cascade. Hard to see though through the mist, growin all the time. No echo yet. He keeps askin questions. Sweat my answers – no no no.

"Sure I don't know you?"

He must be smellin the echo coming. Paralysis answers.

"You got a face just like mine."

Mirror starts sphering. Not good. If I speak things get worse. Start sputtering in the bad way. Syllable salad pours out. Two guys one jack no bueno. Hurts when the mirror starts circling. He's got nothing but confusion on it. Probably never heard of Phroggers. Met one up close. Not good. Bad for both but he ain't worryin cuz he don't know. Can't know. Can't tell him either. Words make it worse. But that mirror curving in on me says too late MF.

"You..." I think he's smellin the PB on me. Confusion thick as the Fog but not feelin good. Starting. He's me. Or thinks he is. The curve gets worse. Total fold. Not good but can't put it into words. He says something, hears himself. I can't.

"Don't touch me!" He come through now.

I'm not touching him but it's started. His words finding my lips. Beads synchronize. In the wall I was safe. Now Krissy's is burning. Our minds touch the flame, just us. Everyone else Fog jacked, perfect obliviousness.

"You..." he mouths the words 'peanut butter' almost connecting but not enough bandwidth. 'you you you you' comin on strong the echo.

Lifts the Fog in a bad way.

He jacks out and I'm stuck.

My body's all his now. At his mercy.

Phrog can't hop.

Don't know what he sees on the outside but Krissy's is a wall of fire. Smoke takes over Fog. I'm coughing.

Lookin down I see ribs snapping.

He's onto me. Too late to unjack.

If only for Fog I could deal.

Back of the neck stings. Hurts. Feels pulled.

Sphere mirror infinity of bad. Inside can't last but curves forever.

Over Night

S tretching his legs Barry knocked over a towering pile of books, stacked so high it was a miracle it hadn't fallen on its own. Looking around his apartment he saw nothing but such piles and his desk which stood empty except for an old manual style typewriter. None of the modern intrusions such as TVs or radios. I'm such a luddite, he thought, unashamed.

Ignoring the books he continued his stretching and preparation for his morning jog. As one who spent most of his time sitting down, either reading or writing, he was getting out of shape. A friend had suggested that he go out and get more exercise, so he took the suggestion to heart and decided to go for a brief run each morning. Today was to be his first and he was glad that the forethought of sore muscles had reminded him to stretch, maybe his legs would hurt that much less.

Opening the door into the bright morning he was greeted by the sound of helicopters overhead, an unpleasant but common sound in the urban environment. He ran up the driveway feeling good about having taken the first steps towards fitness, and wondered how long he would last. Regulating his breathing he sped down the street, enjoying the wind in his hair until his route was thwarted by a red light at the intersection. He jogged in place the way he had seen others do, always thinking that they looked somewhat ridiculous. A black Sedan pulled up next to Barry and the man inside rolled down the window, gesturing to him. Barry, glad for his headphones, pointed to them, and noting the green light, trotted across the street. *I'll never get anywhere if I stop and give directions along the way*, at least that was the first thing that came to mind. Immediately he felt guilty about this. His friend that had suggested the jogging had partly done so under the guise of getting him out of the house. If he was to avoid strangers then part of the reason for the exercise would be moot. Ashamed of his reaction he removed the earbuds and put them in his pocket.

As he crossed the street he noticed people in the waiting cars pointing at him. Was his discourtesy so apparent that others had noticed it? Maybe he had a funny gait, it had been ages since he had gone running. He looked over his shoulder and watched the black Sedan make a U turn, no doubt the fellow was lost looking for the freeway. Feet pounding the pavement he rounded the corner up the street towards the school. The air was filled with the sounds of recess, shouts and laughter, balls hitting chain-link fences. As he approached the playground fell silent and a throng of children pressed themselves up against the gate, all staring at him, none making a sound. Confused and creeped out, Barry picked up speed and did his best to round the next corner as quickly as he could. Rejoicing at reaching the end of the block he almost didn't see a woman with her grocery cart standing at the stoplight, nearly smacking right into her. The look she gave him in return was not one of anger but of awe, almost tinged with a bit of praise. Barry trudged on, baffled. Everyone was acting so strangely, usually people didn't even notice him.

It had only been a few blocks and Barry was starting to feel it in his legs. He knew then that he really was out of shape, for his inner-self had already begun to tell him to return home. Determined, he blocked the thoughts out and continued to run, even picking up the pace a bit. A black Sedan pulled up and drove in pace with Barry. Looking over he saw that it was the same man that had gestured before.

"Mr. President, could I please have a word with you?"

Mr. President? What could this man be thinking? Who does he think I am?

"Wrong guy, buddy." said Barry as he ducked into the foot tunnel that crossed under the freeway. The tunnel always smelled like piss and he had to hold his breath to get through it, but he could never hold it long enough to get all the way to the other side. Taking in a deep breath of the foul air he emerged from the tunnel and took off towards the park. Excited faces in a passing news van stared and pointed at him. When he turned to avoid them two teenagers sitting on the bus stop bench took out their phones and started taking pictures of him. What was this? He couldn't look so ridiculous that even teenagers were interested in him. Several blocks up the street, at the light, Barry saw a black Sedan take the corner, headed his way. Looking the other direction he saw that the news van had also turned and was closing in on him. A wave of anxiety took over and forgetting his fatigue he bounded back into the tunnel. He ran half way through, figuring that both vehicles would be waiting for him on the other side, decided to feint and double back toward the exit that led toward the park. At least this might buy him some time to get away, back to the house. But now he was heading in the opposite direction trying to avoid his pursuers. His fear fueling his muscles.

He saw the teenagers get onto their bus. It seemed that everyone on the crowded public transit was also staring at him, some were even taking pictures. Avoiding the main road he headed up a hill into the residential part of the neighborhood. There were alleys up this way and maybe he could cut through them to get back in the direction of his house. Running up the hill zapped his energy reserves and he was starting to have a hard time regulating his breathing, but he reached the alleyway he was looking for, and it was marvelously free of pedestrians. He made it another two blocks before seeing anyone. A person out walking their dog called out to him and waved. Ignoring them he took advantage of the now downhill slant and picked up speed back towards the freeway. Five blocks to go and he would be safe back at his place. He felt like he needed a breather and looked for a place to hide and rest for a second. Seeing a garbage truck parked next to a wall he decided to hang back between them, just out of sight from the street.

Regaining his composure he jogged back into the street, convincing himself that he was probably just being self conscious about the shape he was in. Making it another block without incident he was now feeling that things might be back to normal. Then he spotted the Sedan, it was several blocks off, but definitely headed toward him. I'm being silly running from this car, the man has obviously just mistaken me for someone else. Resolved to ignore the Sedan and its driver, he headed on in the same direction. Reaching the freeway overpass, and only three blocks from home, Barry was brought to a standstill. The news van screeched up in front of him and blocked his path. He stood frozen as a cameraman and reporter jumped out of the vehicle, both with their sights on him.

The black Sedan parked on the opposite side of the street and Barry felt as if the world was closing in on him. Stepping out of the car a man in a black suit crossed the street in his direction. The reporter and cameraman had set up and were beginning their newscast to his right, freeway behind them as backdrop. Only then did Barry hear the helicopters again. There was a swarm of them above and Barry realized that the sound had never ceased since he had left the house. He looked up to the copters but his gaze was stopped half way as he saw a billboard with his face on it, next to the words "Our Man."

The news camera swung around and pointed at Barry as the newscaster approached him.

"Mr. President, how does it feel to be the world's first head of state elected by lottery?"

Barry didn't hear what she said, or respond. His confusion over the billboard had made him forget about the man in the suit that was now almost on top of him. When he lowered his eyes he caught sight of the man's lapel blown out by the wind, beneath he saw the outline of a pistol. Without thinking he leapt at the man, afraid for his life. The man in the suit and Barry fell to the ground in an awkward embrace. Barry was scrambling for his life, afraid and reacting with animal-like instinct. The man in the suit was trying to subdue him but did not seem intent on causing harm. A gunshot rang out and Barry rolled off of the man and fell dead in the street.

"It went off accidently! I was here to protect him." moaned the man in the suit looking dejected and gaunt.

"Did we get all that on tape?" cried the newscaster. "Keep that camera rolling!" The camera panned to Barry's dead body and then back over to Evelyn the newscaster.

"What started as an amazing day has ended in tragedy. Mr. President, Barry Mitchell, the first president to be elected by lottery, has just been shot in a fatal mix up with the secret service. To date this is the shortest presidential term in our history, and a bad start to the lottery system."

The words were drowned out as sirens began to fill the air. Noting this the camera man panned upward until his lens reached the billboard with the words spelled out, "Our Man."

Come Back Earlier

I 'd made a mess out of the whole damn thing. We never set out to fuck up, but more often than not we do just that. In this case the asinine element was my motivation to do good. "Right the wrongs" I had cried, waving the flag of my own misguided morality. I was no stranger to screwing up, but it had been a long time since I had. My moral compass had been guiding me in the right direction ever since I woke up and realized that I had been an asshole most of my life. Ever since that moment I had made a tremendous effort, slowly at first, until it became a habit to do the right thing and be kind to everyone. Leaving judgment behind is a difficult thing until you're finished judging yourself, your present self that is. The old me would have to remain an asshole in the gutters of the past. At least that's what I thought for a long time, always critical of how I had lived my life. But in my strides toward self-improvement I went back to school and tried to do all of the things that my younger, idiot self, had claimed he wanted to do.

And it was going rather well for a change. I was excelling in school. I had great friends. And it seemed at times that I was truly able to leave behind the life I had lived full of regrets and self loathing. I even smiled on a regular basis. Being kind and solid felt good. When you know your own boundaries you tend to break those of others less frequently. Self-improvement indeed. In less than a decade I'd gone from strung-out deadbeat musician to the scientist I had dreamed of being as a boy. I even met a girl. That didn't pan out as well as some of my other attempts, yet happiness seemed to be within reach, for the first time in my mostly unhappy life.

When I got out of school I got my first real job. One that I wasn't allowed to talk about. With my new set of values it was hard to have to keep a secret from my friends and family. But I was working on real scientific problems, doing something meaningful for the first time in my life. Anyway, they understood and no one held it against me, but they sure were curious and would often tease me about being a secret agent. Little did I know that that was in the cards too. Not espionage by any means, but clandestine, since we couldn't let the world know what we were up to. The government wanted it bad and paid handsomely too. We knew that they would want to weaponize time travel but our team couldn't let ourselves think about that, not with a breakthrough on the way. Not when we were so close to answering one of humankind's greatest questions. And we figured we would find a way to put safe-guards in place, or string the project out and keep our employers in the dark about the real power we had harnessed. So we thought.

They were onto us. It wasn't their first rodeo. Instead of axing us all they brought us deeper into the fold. At this point we were expendable at best. They figured the best way to keep us from talking was to make us the subjects of their clandestine time war. Their rationale was as follows: you made the machine, you did the dirty work. We agreed rather than have our baby stolen from us. And so after-all, through my attempts at self-improvement, and attempts to do something constructive for the world, I was going to have to be an asshole again. Not for self-righteous reasons this time but for what they called "the greater good". Shit, I wasn't a spy and didn't think that I was cut out for the job, but when I told them that they started listing off all kinds of rotten things from my past, assuring me that I was exactly the kind of man they needed for the work at hand.

And so I went back in time and did all kinds of horrible shit. Stuff I would have never thought to do on my own volition. I didn't even want to ask their reasons for some of the tasks they set me to. They wouldn't have told me their rationale anyway. Nor was I allowed to talk to anyone else on the team about what we were doing. The secrecy pained us, we had all set out to do something good and now we were unfit soldiers in a secret time war. A war of which we did not know the reasons or possible outcomes. All my progress towards being a good human being was being undone. For the first time in years I found my self-loathing returning. My hatred of myself grew with every ill deed they bestowed upon me. This awful change inside was not the only effect of our tampering. The changes were subtle, almost imperceptible at first. More homeless on the streets. Things being more expensive, particularly food. They were the types of changes that we've grown jaded to seeing, so it took me a while to catch on to the cause. There was no way to correlate our work to the things I was noticing but my suspicions grew with each minor adjustment.

Revelation snapped inside of me. Things would begin to change exponentially. No matter what the outcome, we didn't have the right to screw with timelines, and didn't know the half of what was really happening. Were we creating alternate universes by creating para-doxes? Did our current world actually change or did we move into new ones? No matter how it was going down it couldn't be right.

Everything inside me spoke up, screamed out, that what we were doing was absolutely wrong. And it was my damned fault. I'd made a mess of everything. Done things that my soul would not be forgiven for. It was beyond hurting people, I'd messed with the fabric of the cosmos itself. I hadn't learned anything. I'd been fooling myself that I understood what empathy meant. But through my self-loathing the answer began to paint itself in lucid clarity. And the opportunity came.

All they wanted of me this time was to divert a pedestrian and make sure they crossed the street at a different intersection. Easy enough. Maybe they didn't want the guy hit by a car or something. Who knows? I had stopped trying to understand their reasoning a long time ago. Little changes could have big effects, and bizarrely big changes could sometimes result in similar outcomes. I stood on the street corner waiting for my mark and thinking about what I had become, then unbecome, then become again, as familiarity rose inside of me. The smell caught me first, a lack luster car wash on a filthy street corner boasting an old banner that read "Re Grand Opening" and had for years. The shriek of bus brakes. The holler of an old drunken veteran down on his luck. I was home. Home twenty years ago. A place I had never liked and fueled my poison like prison mentality. My eyes left my mark and traveled up to the second story of a building half a block down. A pirate flag swayed in the smog. The same Jolly Roger I had flown for years in my pitiful single room that served as cell in those days. It flashed upon me and I knew what to do.

The door only needed a slight kick to open. I never had to worry about forgetting my keys back then. I looked at the old familiar mailbox overflowing with junk mail. The creak of the steps brought back waves of memories. Times I had to drunkenly crawl up the two flights. The swagger of striding up them for the first time to my first place without roommates. The nostalgia evaporated as I passed by a one-time neighbor that acknowledged me but never looked up to see how much older I was. It was easy to believe that decades hadn't happened. I was getting distracted. I had to end this atrocity now. There was no way I could take down the corrupt government that had caused me to blaspheme against causality, but there was something I could do. That kid sitting in that apartment was going to cause all this someday and I had to take him out before he did.

Apartment 108. I was about to knock, then tried the handle instead. I rarely locked the door in those days, that is, if this was before I had my guitar stolen. Apparently it was. The door swung open and I saw him sitting on the small couch in the far corner. A draft of swag weed and cigarettes circled the room. He, or I, didn't even look up as I entered. I knocked the needle off of the record on the turntable. I had long since gotten bored of T-Rex. Only then did he look up, his eyes darkened to shark hue. He got up slowly, looking at me funny the whole time. The look on my face couldn't have been much different. But I was also looking around the room taking in all of the details I had long since forgotten.

I knew I was going to kill him but I hadn't considered how. As he stood up in front of me I realized that I also hadn't considered how different we were. He was a good sixty pounds lighter and mean. Unafraid, he advanced slowly. I stared like a fool. I knew everything about him. He couldn't possibly recognize me and didn't give a damn who I was. I had invaded his space. Still a pet-peeve of mine. He had that look of someone fed up, of someone who had encountered this situation before. And I remembered that indeed he had. My palms clammed up. I hadn't taken into account that I was much more fit in those days. Or that he was steeped in violence in those days and would be ready for me.

I lunged and he gracefully evaded me. I fell into the couch he had just risen from as a cold wave of pain rose up my back from a solid kidney shot. Damage flashed behind my eyes and my stomach turned. I spun around and met his hard gaze. He was smiling but it fell away as my fist found his solar plexus. Breath rushed out of him but he wouldn't go down. He parried with a quick one two. I tasted blood coming from my nose. This little bastard had no idea of the damage he would do. The wounds he was inflicting were nothing compared to his future, my past. My rage melted into clarity. I landed a jab on his mouth. Again he smiled, bringing a knee up into my ribs, which audibly cracked. Now I couldn't breathe and he took full advantage. My mouth opened and closed but took in no air. I was keeled over and I barely saw his signature uppercut coming. Then stars.

Vision returned, first as a dot in the center of blackness, then fading in slowly. He stood above me silently. I grabbed the back of his knee and pulled him down on top of me. We rolled in a death embrace, hands on each other's throats. I released my grip and returned the favor of the kidney blaster. He grunted as his eyes sharpened. I struck again in the same spot and could taste the possibility of besting him. In that moment my confidence cloded my judgment. Could I really beat my younger, harder self? I looked into his eyes and saw the bafflement of recognition. He mouthed something but no words came out, then he brought down his forehead....

Due Date

S he waves her hand over my console and the transaction is complete.

"Thank you, your due date is in three weeks. If you need to renew, feel free to ping me any time before the due date."

Mysterious Island. Not a good sign. It's never a good sign when they check out books about the sea. It means they're lonely. And if they're lonely, they're sad. I do my best to prevent this, by making suggestions, and of course the books we stock. But in the end, I can't tell people what to check out, they have to have at least this freedom. But ocean stories, a bad sign. By now they know when I'm trying to talk them out of a selection, and if I do word will spread and within a month they'll all be reading it anyway, and the sadness will spread crew wide.

It can be worse than that. If they start checking out books about space travel I know there's real trouble. One might think that such books would be a comfort out here, reading about people in similar situations, but from experience I know this to be an act of desperation. It usually means they have forgotten what it's like to be planet bound. When they forget the gravity there's no coming back. If they reach for the sci-fi I have to call the doctor to intervene.

But I've painted a depressing picture. Since I curated the selection before we took off I know the stock really well and can typically make suggestions that help to improve overall morale. There are definitely things I would do differently if I could do it all again though. Like ocean and space books, I would have left those behind if I had known. Something about those great wide-open spaces always spells longing. And that's an emotion that we can't have lingering around on a ship this size. I wonder if when people traveled the world on the actual seas if their librarians faced the same troubles?

I also try to steer them away from the mysteries. One would think that these would be a great pastime while we hurtle through the nothingness with little to do. But I see it almost every time. They start to get suspicious. It's not enough to have the mystery stay on the pages, they begin to doubt their bunkmates, sometimes the entire crew. Makes my job difficult, back home they were such an easy sell for those needing to while away the time.

Non-fiction. That was supposed to be the main thing. After all, we are supposed to be preparing for our new life. I stocked every book on farming, construction, and basically everything we'll need to survive. Not that the folks on this trip don't have tons of skills like that, but we're due to get rusty after all these years of inactivity. No matter how much I try to push these subjects, no one wants to hear it. The thought of soil in their hands is almost as bad as thinking about the sea, or space. The reminders of home drag my shipmates right out of the present and back to darker times. One would think that picturing a tree in your mind would be a peaceful affair, but it's just another reminder of what we're leaving behind, and the uncertainty to which we travel.

"Do you have another copy of Mysterious Island?"

The question draws me out of my contemplative state. And so it's begun to spread. The infection of the mind, missing those oceans, all that water, and shrinking at the thought of where we're going, and all of the things it might lack.

"It's checked out at the moment. How about something educational?"

They're gone before I can hand them a book. The non-fiction route almost never works. Still, I have to try. It's understandable that they don't want the reminders, but we had better be ready when we arrive, even though that's a decade away. That's a long time not to hone one's trade. Even longer not to be thinking about the work. For most of us our arrival seems so far away, and it is, but if we start to slip now there's no telling how bad things could get in the remaining time of the journey. At least for the moment everyone is still doing their ship duties. But Mysterious Island... I may need to speak to the Captain.

What books would I have brought if I had known what I know now? It's hard to say. I am comforted by the books themselves. Even just the smell of them calms me. That's why we decided to bring physical books. Something about having the real object makes us feel more connected to those who wrote them. Or that's what we thought. It still works for me, but I wonder if I'll fall victim to the same malaise that's infecting the crew. I've got to think of some new titles to recommend, something to help get them out of this funk.

Typically, when all else fails, I would divert to the classics. Now I know that won't work either. In the early days of our trip I tried that, but the pacing was all wrong for everyone. Our trip is a slow one, so nobody wanted to read slow books about fanciful people that can move around at their leisure. No one was reading much in those days anyway, the boredom had yet to set in, everyone was still excited about our new lives and our upcoming adventures. Nothing like years of routine to get the restlessness going. Eventually everyone took to reading voraciously but it didn't last. No one was interested in a book club. I guess the idea came off as stuffy, and no one was reading the same titles anyway. That was before the patterns started to emerge.

No requests have come in but I'm starting to wonder if we should have brought along some self help books. Though they would probably be embarrassed about checking those out. Knowing what books the crew reads can be an intimate thing. Anyway, I didn't bring many.

The looks the crew give me are a clear indicator that they too are disappointed with my selection. And they are not pleased when they sense my reluctance to check out their requests. If only they knew that I am trying to protect them from the dreaded malaise. How could I have known before being out here myself. I am afflicted with the same dangerous mindsets, but I can't let anyone see that I am troubled, it would only make things worse and further interfere with the trust put in my position.

If I could do it all over again, I would have brought magazines. Something light that makes people feel connected with the goings on of the world, rather than the lonely places and dramas. Information that can be taken in in bite-sized pieces without the commitment of time that goes along with a novel. Our job, at this point, is mainly to wait, so the crew feels the passage of time in a painfully slow fashion. If I had brought more cheap entertainment perhaps they would have something to discuss with one another that avoids the more brutal aspects of our position. I think it might have worked. I wish I had known. Maybe the idea of something disposable would have been appealing to them, something we don't have to recycle over and over again.

Or should I have brought audiobooks? These days everyone that comes to the library seems to have an aversion to conversing with me. If I had stocked audiobooks it would have brought along with it a whole cast of stranger's voices. I think it's the sound of my voice that makes them cringe, along with the fact that most of my job consists of fairly scripted dialog. The audiobooks could have spoken to them, introduced a slew of foreign voices that no one has had the time to grow sick of. But now I'm speculating, and it won't do the crew any good to think about what could have been, what I could have brought, or what I could have done better. It's too late for that.

But it occurs to me that perhaps it's not the material that's the problem. It could be that the act of reading is solitary. Everyone feels alone and I'm giving them one more reason to be alone. I think back to all those smiling faces of the children at the terrestrial library during story time and realize that that's what we've been missing all the while. We need to read together, to go through the stories together. Perhaps it's not the stories of the sea, mysteries, or sci-fi, but the fact that we need to face our loneliness together.

So, I'm not going to worry about what books people check out, reading should always be a good thing. Instead, I'm going to put out a notice that tomorrow evening the ship's library will be hosting our first adult story time read along. Doing something fun together should raise the spirits of the crew, and we can face our loneliness together for a change.

Western Expansion

You see, one too many people stepped on my back. Most of them didn't notice their footprints. How they took weeks, or more, to decay. Slowly weathering, softening at the edges. I like things spread out. Every life has its own space. At least a few feet anyway. We do this for good reason. You get hit by lightning, I don't burn. I get hit, you go free. In the forest one tree burns, they all do. Here we have sand and space to protect us from the wildfire. We're a slow grow, and a slow burn. You ain't gettin' close, even if you're fire, cuz we've spread in the aesthetic way. Alone beauty.

But the footprints they left us. Started closing the spaces. Giving lightning a chance. They left things to burn between us. Footprints that lasted longer than they imagined. Concrete doesn't allow for footprints. They live where people will come and change it for them. They don't wait for the wind like we do. So to show them I asked the wind to move west from now on. If they'd been further east they'd know that the sands continue, change color, but go on and on. The wind didn't mind, I asked politely.

It blew. West and west. Took the sands with it too. Hallowed the footprints in a different way this time. Me and my plants weren't used to the shift. Things had remained the same since the mountains were made. Now my grains flowed back towards the ocean. My plants will live. Some of them have been here since before I dried things out. Now, I'm coming west, to suck the moisture out of you. But I asked the wind to go first and she did, reversing the ages in a way that you might not be ready for. She told you to come visit, but she didn't tell you that your tent was gonna knock your ass around as you pretended it was an apartment in the city.

First we drank. Then we powdered. From now on you won't have to be swallowed by Amboy Crater. I'm coming to you. The winds take me to Redlands. I reclaim. Then the rest of San Bernardino County. I take Riverside. I take Los Angeles. The sands come with me. Your parking lots become dune fields. Sand drifts cover your sidewalks. From now on your boots will be as dusty as ours. High heels are a thing of the past. I move onward west until my sands meet with those of the ocean. At last, after millennia, I reach the sea again. The dry winds blow away all moisture and sound can now travel miles as your smog blows outward, always farther west.

Gardens shrivel. The barrel cactus you stole from me will be amongst the only plants to survive. I'm bigger than I was and my appetite has grown with me. I drink your lakes, your rivers and creeks, and eventually I will drink your sea. Freeways sway in the wind as the visibility dissipates. Traffic thickens as the wind blows cars off course and the sandstorms splay the paint from your cars. Traffic so thick it will stop the eastward migration. Don't come to me, I have come to you. So have the carrion birds, see them circling overhead. They await you to run over my mice and rats. All the creatures head westward. Open your hood they have eaten the electronics from your vehicle.

Your car overheats. Your AC overheats. Triple digits fend you back towards the ocean as well. But I have boiled your seas.

Concrete. Concrete everywhere. It raises my temperature. Nothing to cool me down. Your streets will disappear in my sands as you wish that the mountains of asphalt were not on my side, aiding me in raising the mercury. The streets crack, unused to my heat. Manicured lawns brown. Bird baths dry up. Pools empty into the sky, water replaced by sand. When you think you see water it's me playing tricks on you. The air itself is boiling. Sea breezes have changed direction forever, head west to join the others, never again to cool the coast which I have commandeered. The rain shadow descends upon you as we become one.

Scorpions, snakes, and centipedes join me in my westward march. You become afraid to walk barefoot. You do not know to shake out your boots. You thought things would be clean and you could come to my haunts to "rough it." By "rough it" you meant leave trash, dog shit, and drain my waters rinsing off after your Airbnb Jacuzzi time. I've seen your groups drink, shower, and hose away five thousand gallons in a weekend. Even the parasitic tamarisk trees can't do that kind of damage. So now I'm here to drink your pools dry. Replace the water you stole with sand, always sand. Even your trash-fed coyotes run for what was once the shore, afraid of the heat hardened real thing.

How do your feet feel upon my back now? Now that it's your backyard too, and you'll be forced to live as those whom you drove out with your property values and your vacations and your polluting migrations on the weekends. Trash mixed up in a tumbleweed enters your once glistening green gardens. It's a popsicle wrapper, the same you let fly from your window after pausing to take a picture with my iconic trees. The dog shit is easier to see against the backdrop of my golden sands. It dries, powders, then joins the air. My winds take them and spread the flotsam for all to breathe.

The Southwest is mine. More so than before. Come visit, you won't have to travel far. Now we share a back, so go ahead and tread. I will adapt to the invasive species, now they have been invaded too. My dust will crawl up your boots, coat your tires, and join you in the living room. The winds change your tides and will heed to none. Blowing eternally. I have made plenty of room for your development. Try to tame me, building endlessly. I will grow as you do, remaining a step ahead. When your sprawl reaches between the great oceans, a continuous stretch, I will have come first. I will spill across the plains taking the rains away as I go. If you try to suck me dry, know that I have already done it for you. Know that my sands record history, which seems so fleeting to you, but is permanent. You will learn to read this record. You will have to see it throughout the days.

Free Download

"I'm glad that you came in today, Richard. A man at the cross-roads of life, such as yourself, needs to start planning his future beyond the corporeal state. I know what you are going to say... Is it the same as the here and now? The answer is no, but, and this is a big but, it is definitely not death. Not in the old fashion sense of the word anyway. And again, it's great that you came in today, because I can give you a firsthand demonstration of what I mean."

"That's great, because that's actually why I came in. You see my family has been bugging me to do this ever since my daughter got pregnant, for some reason they think I might not be around to get to know my grandkids. They keep telling me that this is the next best thing. I guess I'm old fashioned, but the idea of it seems kind of crazy to me."

"Richard, I understand. A lot of people feel the same way you do at first. You know, most people think that if you can't touch something , that it doesn't exist. But ask yourself, can you touch love, can you touch your soul? Of course not, but we know that they are both real. In a sense that is what we are able to preserve here at Bionetics

International, those intangible things that are the real meaning of life."

"So what exactly happens, and is there a guarantee that it will work? I mean, will I feel anything?"

"I'm glad you asked because I was just coming to that. First we'll do a body scan and have you respond to a series of questions. This is merely to preserve your image, that way if your family feels more comfortable interacting with you in association with your image, all they have to do is switch on the holoprojector and it will be like you are there with them in the room. We have many other interface solutions, but the holoprojector is by far our best selling accessory. After the body scans we'll move on to the neural network mapping. This is where the real magic happens. By creating a virtual analog of your synaptic pathways and interactions we are able to build a perfect reproduction of your consciousness. From there your input and output must all enter your mind via computer interface, but in reality it is the only noticeable difference from living inside of your body. And it is totally safe, should you decide that you don't like this form of afterlife, all you have to do is ask to be disconnected. The procedure is painless, in fact pain will be a thing of the past for you, and it is all completely at your discretion."

"All right, that all sounds pretty good, but still kind of too good to be true. How will I know that I will still be me, how will I know that what my family is getting isn't some kind of abomination, or just a computer program?"

"Again, Richard, I'm glad you asked. The best method, tried and true, is for you to see for yourself. What we are going to do, free of charge for a great client like yourself, is give you a live demonstration. If you wouldn't mind stepping inside of the scanning room and following the prompts, you'll be able to meet with yourself and ask all the questions you like. Right this way."

***

"I must say that that was the most eerie moment of my life. I'm convinced now that my family would have a hard time telling the difference, but I cannot help but feel that what you have shown me is not me. I don't think anyone else could tell the difference, but there's just something off about it to me."

"I hate to tell you this, Richard, but the reason he seems off to you is because you are not the same person you were when we took the scans. The experience of meeting yourself has changed you, and this is quite common. The way around it is simple. We take regular scans for the remainder of your corporeal life and keep the virtual you up to date."

"I can't go through with this, I'm sorry I wasted your time. Your service just isn't for me. Thanks for the demonstration."

"All right, Richard, if you say so. I'll go ahead and delete the files. Please let us know if you change your mind. We also offer family deals if your wife should want to give it a try."

"Thanks, I'll let her know. Before I go, what happens to me, I mean to the demonstration, when you delete the files?"

"The virtual you just ceases to exist, that's all. Don't worry, he won't feel a thing." "Wait a minute! First you try to sell me eternal life, and now you are going to kill me?"

An Off the Record Letter to the People Watching Back Home

Everyone knows that it takes a long time to get anywhere traveling through space. Even at light speed the trips are loooong. You see pictures of us spinning in circles, catching floating globes of water. You think that's all we do? Now you imagine us standing around consoles, turning knobs and watching blinking lights. Geez, you've seen too many movies. How many hours of the day do you think we spend on that kind of crap? Well, I can tell you, while I have turned some knobs and flicked some switches in my life, computers are better suited for this work. We're mostly here to prove it's possible. To see if we can really leave and eventually stay somewhere. We look for paradise in the ever greatening darkness.

Anyway, we still have lives and do regular stuff. In fact, most of our days are much like yours, with the exception that we probably put in more hours. The main difference is that there is no privacy. Tight quarters at best. The endless noise of the machines covers up voices if you let it. But we are almost never outside of visual contact with each other.

The TV is fond of saying that we eat together, that bonding at mealtime and close proximity is good for the psyche. That's the TV friendly version anyway. Yeah, we do that, but that's not all. We can leave for the stars but we can't leave human needs behind. We bring all that stuff with us. What do you see in your mind's eye now? I'll bet all-of-a-sudden you started thinking about space flight as boring. Obviously you don't know us very well. Don't worry it's not your fault. The propaganda, the radio dispatches they let you hear, and those dumb films of us eating water out of the sky – yeah, it all makes us look pretty apple pie. Do you really think that would work? It wouldn't.

While our daily activities are much the same as yours, we can't go anywhere. And there is NO privacy. I can see you shuddering now. For us it's no problem. The solution was simple. Our crew, and they don't want you to know this, is polyamorous. We're all exhibitionists and voyeurs. The lack of privacy can be a real turn on. And when we're done twiddling knobs for "education" videos we're busy with a healthy and vigorous sex life. Don't feel like joining in? Go ahead and watch.

Now you're seeing million dollar money shots in your head. Calm down. Strict protocol for stuff like that. But we're active. Wouldn't you be if you had so much time to kill? None of the crew discriminate much, keeps us from getting bored or developing resentments. A little of this, a little of that. But you won't see that in the films. They don't want you to know your tax dollars lead to so much fun, and all without American values. After-all , we're about as far from America as you can get.

Blue Gemini One

"Blue Gemini One, your orbit has stabilized. Please run protocol sequences while we test the communications relays. We'll be moving from direct transmission to scrambled satellite relay. You'll be cut off for a minute, sit tight while we reconfigure the carrier waves. Mission Control out." The Navy man's voice clicked off.

Branson ran the sequences while allowing himself to focus on the strange effects of zero G. The view through the capsule's window was majestic, a sight reserved for the chosen few. Blinking lights on the control panel drew his attention away from the bright blue globe and back to the mission. A crackle of static spilled out of his headset then faded.

They must be having issues down there, or with the satellite ricochet. Coms should have been reestablished by now. "Control are you reading me? Had a moment of static there, but I could not read you. Everything going alright down there?"

Silence rang through the capsule's cockpit. The lack of response made the craft feel even smaller. While the original Gemini capsule had been designed for two, the Navy's Blue Gemini capsules had been modified for small satellite transport, making them less spacious. Branson's legs were pressed up against the control panels. He was too hot, but checking the dials he found that cabin temperature had remained consistent. He flipped the UHF switches to see if he could get Control back on the unencrypted channels. Nothing.

The abort button called out to him. *It's too soon for that. Damn this mission being secret. If only I could raise Houston, or even a civilian facility. Priorities, Branson. Maybe something is wrong with my audio output.*

Branson opened the Audio 1 panel below the O2 gauge. His engineer mind followed the circuit paths. Nothing seemed out of order. He reset the device and positioned it back in place. He moved the lever and put his mirror in the open position. Nothing was behind him. *At least it's not a Red satellite trailing me, or something worse.*

His shoulders tensed as he tried transmitting again. *Maybe they can hear me. Perhaps it's a malfunction on my end.* Still no response. A full communications blackout. *It's been twenty five minutes. This is taking way too long. I'm out here without provisions. This mission is supposed to be wrapped up within the hour.* The dull gray of the cockpit paneling blurred into a cage. A cage that could become a coffin.

He longed to stretch his legs out. To walk, not in space but on solid ground. He longed for voices. In return he heard the dull hiss of his air circulation systems. Still no response from Control. *They must know something is wrong. I already put out the distress call. What if they are getting static on their end too? Blue Gemini Two isn't scheduled for another six months. There won't be a rescue mission.*

This last thought filled him with dread. He could think of nothing except the abort button. "The Shame Switch" they had jokingly called it. He looked out the small window again as he whispered a prayer to the great cosmos outside, as his trembling hand floated up towards the red lit rectangular button that would end his last mission.

Homo Paniscus

S he crossed the Columbia River and headed up I-5 towards the laboratory. Sherry hated Mondays. It was not that she didn't like her job, in fact she loved her work, but she was not a morning person and after sleeping in all weekend getting up on Monday could be hell. The bridge brought her from Portland into Vancouver. She always found it kind of funny that she worked in one state and lived in another, but once off the main highway and past the first town in Washington the forest opened up and the drive became beautiful, especially this time of year. The facility was off of the beaten path for several reasons, mainly because people reacted poorly to the work they were doing, but also to deter guests. Sherry pulled into a parking spot, looked herself over in the rear-view mirror, and got out her security badge to check in for work.

After checking in Sherry made her way down the corridor to the lab. Before arriving she could tell that something odd was going on today, people ran around the hallways in seeming disarray. By the door to her office she saw her boss, Dr. Greene, speaking with the police.

She hadn't noticed their cars outside. She must have been more tired than she thought.

"Ah, Sherry, there you are, no one's probably told you yet, but we had a break-in last night." said Dr. Greene, looking disappointed.

It was not wholly unusual for the police to visit the laboratory, several times in the past activist groups had come to protest their work, and one time they had tried to break in to free the animals.

"Oh my god! Are the bonobos all right?" Sherry's first concern was always for the animals that she worked with directly. After years in the lab she had grown quite close with some of them.

"Yes, they all appear OK, you'll have time to give them a full check-up soon, unfortunately this disruption will set us back. The police would like to have a word with you, then we can get started making sure about the animals, and that there is no damage to the lab." said Dr. Greene before thanking the policeman and handing the conversation over to her.

The policeman looked at her warmly and began, "Very sorry to interfere with your work day, Miss Allen, I just have a few questions for you then we'll be out of your way."

***

"There you are, Jimbo. Did you have an exciting night? Have you been behaving yourself?" said Sherry to the large male bonobo while scratching his head down the part in his hair.

Jimbo squirmed in the pleasure of being pet and responded with nothing else. She spent a few moments with him, making sure that he was not behaving unusually. When she was satisfied that his emotional state was normal she moved down the row of cages to Tina, the dominative but social female bonobo of the group. Tina sat quietly in the corner of her cage and at first ignored Sherry as she approached. Immediately Sherry began to worry, typically Tina was ecstatic to see her and had difficulty containing it. Today's reaction was one that Sherry had never seen before,

"Tina, honey, are you OK little one?" Sherry spoke Motherese while slowly advancing on the cage.

It took over an hour before Tina returned to acting the way that she usually did. At first the creature seemed weary of the humans, but warmed up as familiar faces joined Sherry in the room. The scientists on staff in the bonobo research department were starting to think that perhaps the intruder from the weekend's break-in had done some-thing to Tina, but they would need to wait before doing any tests to find out. It would be a risk to put the animal through two major stresses in a row. So it was decided to go about the daily routine with the animals and give Tina a full checkup later in the week.

Sherry took it upon herself to cheer Tina up and spoiled her with games and fruit treats, almost to the point where the other animals were starting to notice and demand treats of their own. The bonobos were stirred into activity easily, especially if one of them instigated the others. Jimbo wanted more fruit and started hollering, which ignited the others to do the same. Tina looked confused by all of this and Sherry wished that she could remove the animal to a quieter, more private place.

***

"Look idiots. If you want to join this Greek, you are going to have to prove a lot of things. Not just your manhood, not just your grades, but you are going to have to prove that you are not afraid." shouted Jerry, one of the older guys at the house. Jerry was a business major and was in his third year at the University of Portland. He faced a group of freshmen that stood lined up against the basement wall, staring blankly and awaiting their instructions. The house that Jerry was part of had a reputation for some of the highest grades on campus, and for some of the most brutal hazing.

Luke, an anthropology major, joined in, "Each of you will be pre-scribed a different task, one that will be given to you in secret, one that needs to be carried out in secret, one that will prove your loyalty to this fraternity." He exchanged glances with Jerry and both of them paused to add dramatic effect to the ritual.

The guys of the house had thought long and hard about what the newbies would have to go through, and had come up with elaborate ways for them to prove themselves. Part of their plan had been hatched while they were having an argument about creationism. Jerry, who had grown up Catholic, believed in evolution, but suspected that its mechanism was God's doing in some way. Luke, who was neck deep in anthropological studies, suggested that there was an easy way to settle the debate once and for all. Many had considered it, but none had dared. All one would have to do is artificially inseminate a supposed close relative to humans. If we truly are related species, then it follows that such a union would produce a mule.

The conversation had started innocently enough, but soon moved to the dubious idea of using the new batch of freshmen to try out such an experiment. Luke stole, or borrowed as he called it, a security pass from a fellow student who was interning at the primate lab just up north. They made one of the newbies masturbate into a bag, not telling him what it was for. Two of the others they sent with a needle-less hypo to the labs with specific instructions that this activity would never be discussed outside of the small circle.

***

After a few days it was finally considered safe to run Tina through a battery of tests. Her stress levels must have subsided for she was behaving the way she usually did. Sherry went through all of the physical response tests first, knowing that Tina would be more apt to do them before the blood-work. She passed the tests with flying colors and Sherry was convinced that the bonobo was at least in good physical condition. She then strapped the creature in for x-rays and blood tests. The animal clearly didn't like being strapped in but was fairly used to the procedure and didn't struggle too much.

When the results came in Sherry was beside herself, nothing about the results made sense. She picked up the telephone and dialed, unsure of how to present the situation, "Dr. Greene, I have, well, some strange news to relay." Sherry paused knowing that this was probably not going to go well, "I have just received the results from the blood-work concerning Tina. I'm not quite sure how to explain this but... Well, it seems that she is pregnant."

"What!" said Dr. Greene on the other end of the line.

"I know, Doctor, it seems impossible, none of the animals have been allowed contact with each other for months. I believe that one of two things has happened, either our intruders let the animals mate, or we have a parthenogenesis on our hands." Hard to believe as it was, the latter seemed more plausible since the animals would have been impossible to handle for anyone but a professional.

There was silence on the line for a minute and then finally Greene spoke, "That is extremely peculiar, are you sure the results are correct? I heard about the parthenogenic shark a few years back, but could it really be possible in primates?" The disbelief in his voice was impossible to mask.

***

Seven months later Tina started experiencing major problems with the pregnancy. She still had a month to go before the baby was supposed to come, but it was looking like it would be a premature birth. All throughout the pregnancy there had been complications, and all along the scientists attributed them to the parthenogenic conception. Now, expecting a premature birth they did an internal probe to see if the baby would be healthy. What they found shocked them to the core.

"Sherry, I suppose that you have seen the recent charts on Tina's baby? Do you have any suggestions to offer? I really hate to imply this, but do you think someone from the lab could have done this? Who in their right mind would do such a thing?" Dr. Greene rambled out the questions as though there was no end to them, "If foul play is indicated, which I believe it is, then this lab could be in serious trouble, possibly even at risk of being closed down. This could be the biggest human rights disaster in the history of scientific research." Greene was deeply shaken and not bothering to hide it.

Sherry was at a loss for words, sadness and revulsion exuded from her. More than anything else she felt horrible for Tina. The bonobo would most likely die from the premature birth, the baby was just too big for her little body. "At least we have an explanation for what happened the night of the break-in last year." It was the only positive thing to say that she could come up with.

"This is probably going to be the end of us, the animal rights activists are going to have a field day when this gets out. Sherry, I need to know, seriously, what are the chances of terminating the pregnancy?" Dr. Greene's face took on a grave expression, adding to the seriousness of the matter.

"Dr. Greene! You should know as well as I do that it is way too late for such measures. And on top of that it would be highly immoral, that child is at least partly human. Are you really suggesting that we kill it?" Sherry was shocked by the grim way he was talking.

"It is not human, it is an abomination, a cruel act against nature, we have to do something." The hysterics in his voice were becoming more and more obvious.

Sherry was shaken by the fear in the man's voice and became defensive, "It may not be human, but its father surely is. Perhaps we should look at this the other way around. At least now we have proof of our theory that humans evolved from chimpanzees."

Night/Day

N ight

  I was in his body again. She was lying next to his body. I feared to stir knowing she was always cranky when woken in the middle of the night. I could see her soft face in the glow of the nightlight. It looked so peaceful and young. It was, this was probably somewhere near the beginning, when things were still good. I could feel that he desperately needed sleep. It must have been going on for quite some time because his massive headache was now mine. I needed water but didn't feel like I could get up on account of her, so I rolled over and gently put my arms around her. Oh, it was good. Her supple body in my arms once again. It was as if the years hadn't passed me by after all. I kissed her neck as she stirred, careful not to wake her but drinking her in as much as I could in our one-way embrace.

  Back in my time morning came and I watched the sunrise tired with sagging eyes. Moistened eyes filled with regret. And all the pain was back. My neck hurt like hell, only matched by my fatigue from being up most of the night. The house was empty as it always was. An air of cold clung to the walls and furniture even though it was mid-summer. Everything was as it always was, my cold lonely house.

***

Day

"You look tired again today. Are you still not sleeping well?" asked Janet. There was a tinge of annoyance in her concern today. We started off most days this way, at least we had been for a few months now.

"Yeah, I think I was tossing and turning all night, again. The pills don't seem to be working. I don't think I have had a decent night's sleep in weeks. Sorry if I've been keeping you up too."

Again with that tone. "Don't worry about me. You should start exercising like the doctor told you, you know it's supposed to help with insomnia."

I didn't bother replying. She knew well that I had been jogging at least every other day like my doctor had suggested. But like everything else that the doctor, or friends, or family had told me I should do, none of it seemed to have any effect. I just couldn't get more than four hours of sleep in a night.

***

Night

Again the pain was gone. God being young was a relief. I looked at her, again in the soft glow of the nightlight. She looked so beautiful while she slept, at peace, untarnished by the annoyances of the daytime. Even the way her lip hung slightly limp was appealing to me. Why had I taken her for granted in those days? I wanted to wake her and kiss her passionately but knew that she would probably push me away and groan in her little way. Or was this still earlier, before things had started getting bad. I wish there was an easier way to see at what point in our relationship this was, but I entered him at random. I could get up and look at the calendar but the fear of disturbing her terrified me. For all I knew it would be the last time I saw her, and I couldn't bear that being a negative experience again. So, I lie there trying not to move as I do night after night.

She does that little whimper that means she might talk in her sleep. Usually it's incoherent nonsense but I need to hear her voice. Occasionally she wakes up and says something, usually telling me to go back to sleep. I long for a kind word. I can only hope it is the beginning and she has one for me. I want to wake her and ask but instead I wait to hear if she will speak in her sleep. She murmurs then turns over and I can no longer see her face.

***

Day

When I wake up she is already gone off to work. Mornings are often like this. She let me sleep through the alarm knowing that I was probably up through the night. I am unsure if she does this to let me get what little sleep I can or if she doesn't want to speak with me because I have interfered with her rest as well. I catch sight of my face in the mirror as I brush my teeth. My cheeks sag and large black circles ring my eyes. I look haggard and wonder if she can keep loving me in this state.

I find a note on the coffee table. "I'll be out late with the girls tonight. Don't wait up for me. I'll try not to wake you on my way in."

Doesn't she know that I want to see her? I live in a fog day and night, she is the only light that shines through that mist. I can watch her while she sleeps but the nights are unclear to me, half dream of the future, half blur of abstract nonsense. God my neck is stiff from not sleeping. I hope it doesn't get worse.

***

Night

His body is not as pain free as it usually is. Still, its pain is nothing compared to my "present" state. How we take for granted the youthfulness of body. His body is as pain free as her body is beautiful. She smells slightly of alcohol as if she had gone to bed late after drinking. She snores pleasantly. How I missed that sound. How easy it is to stare at her all night. Even though she didn't wash her makeup before retiring to bed, and I never liked makeup, her beauty still overwhelms me. What a fool I was to let us grow apart. This feeling does away with my restraint and I wake her gently with a nudge.

She turns over and mumbles, looking into my face. I wonder if she can tell my soul is older inside his body. She breathes out some sweet unintelligible word as I gasp at the sound of her voice, so foreign and familiar all at once. I cannot remember the last time she actually spoke to *me*. Her lovely chime of a voice actually lulls me to sleep. If only for a moment longer.

***

Day

"You were actually asleep when I came home last night. Did you sleep the whole night through?" asks Janet.

"I did pass out early. But I'm not sure if I stayed asleep. It's been getting hard to tell. When you spend so much time staring at a dark wall all of the nights start to blend."

I can see the disappointment in her face and I get the sudden wave of anxiety that screams at me that she perhaps met someone else last night. I want to ask but revert to cowardice. I almost reach for her hand, stop myself and give into a fear that will bring future sleepless nights. I watch her leave for work. Neither of us said goodbye. I have the day off to sulk.

My aches are accumulating. The fog doesn't lift and I know that it is making me come off self absorbed. I know I am not sleeping but cannot seem to remember the nights. If only I could get use to them.

***

Night

I don't know if being pain free is the best thing, or if it is being next to her. Tonight she has left the nightlight off so I can't see her face but my hands meet her curves with a welcome feeling. Her body responds to my touch. I'm fully alert now. And aroused. I don't know how many of my nights I have lain here, for the second time, each of these nights twice. Ever grateful for a second time with her. All I want to do is make love to her. Somehow it feels wrong. And so right. I wish she would wake up and talk to me.

I stretch out, frustrated. At least I can soak up the aches being gone for the moment. Every time I return to my "present" self the pain seems worse. The moments of respite are a harsh contrast to how I usually feel. What a heavy mix of pleasure and want. No wonder I couldn't sleep in those days, these days. The need for her is causing a restlessness that is difficult to articulate.

***

Day

Janet looks kind of angry. "You kept me up through the night pawing at me." "I'm sorry. You know I do that in my sleep sometimes. I don't think I can help it."

Her face stern. "Well, you know I have an important meeting at work today. Your timing is horrible. If you want to make love to me don't wait until the middle of the night. You have to stop making your sleeplessness my problem or we'll have to get separate beds."

I can't tell if she is fully serious or if this last statement is in jest. I fear to ask. I don't remember groping her last night. I can barely remember anything about my sleepless nights. Why must my problems always create more problems?

The door slams. She must have been serious. Lost in my thoughts I didn't even get to say goodbye. I would have preferred to smooth things out before she left, but I guess I blew it twice in a row. I hope the meeting goes ok, I can't stand the thought of her still being in a mood when she returns from work.

***

Night

Ah, the relief. I let it sink in for a minute. My hand moves towards her but falls empty on the bunched up covers. I turn to look at what I think will be an empty space but see her bundled up on the edge of the bed. Usually she slept next to me. Is this a meaningful distance? Or has she too been tossing and turning? I pull her closer to me and she lets out a slight, pleasurable moan. I take it as a sign and now I'm aroused again.

I wait frozen, unsure if I should follow through. His, my, body is mad with desire. God I wish I knew if this was the beginning, middle, or end. Back then I would have known if it was the right time. Or would I have? Reason has a way of fleeing in these circumstances. I inch towards her, wanting to wake her and trying not to at the same time. It takes hours to find her body.

Now I am pressed up against her and she responds in kind. She is limp in my arms but responds to my touch pleasantly. She tenses in a good way, in rhythm with my touch. It makes me feel brave and I kiss her on the mouth. She doesn't wake but returns my kiss. I caress her belly and thighs. Still asleep it is now obvious that she is aroused, I'm no longer alone in my passion. She opens to me and I enter her. How many years has it been?

By the time I finish she is fully awake. Her beautiful eyes meet mine.

"What's different about you?" she says, "You're not the same."

***

Day

"What got into you last night? I know there's something weird going on and I don't appreciate your behavior. I told you to stay off of me in the middle of the night." There is bitterness in her voice.

"I don't remember anything happening, what are you talking about?"

"First you pull that shit and now you can't even remember. You're losing it aren't you. Don't drag me down just because you can't keep it together. You better treat me with some respect from now on. Get it together if you don't want to mess this up. I'm sick of this crap."

"I'm, I'm sorry. I really don't remember, Janet. Please don't take that tone with me, you know it scares me. I'm trying to get it together, I just need a good night's sleep every now and then. I'll go see the doctor again. I'll fix this. I swear."

***

Night

Again I'm lying awake. The nightlight is off again. His, my, head hurts. The sleeplessness must be catching up with him. Does that mean this is towards the end? Despite the headache his body still hurts a lot less than mine does. I'll take a headache anytime over the impossible pains all over my neck, joints, and back.

I want her again. Last night, my last night anyway, was not enough. How did I let her slip away years ago? She was all I ever wanted. She was how I wanted to spend the rest of my days. She was the bliss that has evaded me in this life. She left me, but at least I can revisit these nights and pretend that all that never happened. That we lived a happy life together, and my nights sleepless or otherwise, were spent by her side.

But she isn't here. I am alone in bed. I get up and look out the window, but it isn't my present. I'm still in his body, in his apartment. But she isn't sleeping in the bed, or on the couch. She simply isn't here. And it hits me. This is the night she left me for good.

***

Day

When I wake up Janet isn't beside me. I'm groggy as hell and wonder where the hours went. I know I couldn't have slept much. I feel it in my bones. But again I have no recollection of the hours spent awake staring at the ceiling. I drag myself to the kitchen, strong coffee on my mind. Next to the percolator I find her note.

"Dear John..."

Night Patrol

He's six years old.

A ninja.

Black pants and sweatshirt, he slips the ski mask over his face, checks the mirror as he slides dad's big boy machete into the belt, tying the impression together into one fear ridden pulp. In the mirror he sees insanity no superhero buglers would cower from, but a maniacal parody – frightening due to the paradox it must instill on would be intruders. One more door check. Patrols.

Masked prowlers, aliens, dinosaurs circle the perimeter. Testing the blade, speed is not on his side. It's heavy. Dog snarls and far off broken bottles disturbs the air. Every creak is an enemy. Ninjas aren't supposed to be this afraid. Tremulous, sword reenters scabbard – he'll grow if he has to. Craziness is large. He's seen it before. The unexpected can fend off the bad guys. Surprise too – and laughter. They'll get scared too if they don't understand. Turning a bunch of lights off he becomes one with the shadows. The moon promises werewolves.

Time stands still in the room, but outside men and monsters move at quicker paces. Ninja makes his way under the couch, shrinking back down to size. Invaders won't see but a well-timed strike could sever tendons and bring them down... if there's only one of them... if he can swing the blade just right while lying down flat on his stomach – it's not a good striking pose.

The hours pass, he's supposed to be in bed. Hours. Beasts still lurk outside. Soon though, so will parents. Ninja removes the uniform. Carefully places the sword back in its resting place, and dons pajamas, leaps into bed. Sound at the door. Now protectionless he feints sleep, doorknob turns. Parents arrive home from date night. No babysitter awaits, only a scared boy pretending to sleep.

We Are Not Safe Here

A TRIBUTE TO PHILIP K. DICK

R ichard picked up the finished manuscript and placed it in the safe. He turned the dial and left the room, locking his door on the way out. He headed down the driveway and across the unmowed lawn, then got into his beater and headed off for the store.

***

Shaking his head Martin awoke to the sound of the clicking of the safe knob. He could feel the woozy after effects of M-Jel. His head swam in disorientation. He had no idea where he was. Martin took two steps forward and tripped over a soft body that squealed gently as he fell onto it. Finding a flashlight in his pocket he turned it on and realized that he had tripped over a young woman. Two other bodies were emerging from unconsciousness and writhed with post-trip moans.

"Where did you people come from?" demanded Martin

The woman he had tripped over replied, "I was just getting off the bus. I was fleeing my hometown, I don't know why I would've ended up here."

Now standing, a man named Nicholas came forward. "Why are you asking all the questions? You tell me what I'm doing here. You don't want to be caught messing with me, I know some folks that you would not like to meet."

The other man that had not yet spoken now did. "Hey, hey, let's not get all worked up here. My name is Raymond and I don't know what I'm doing here either. For now it's good that we at least have a little light. Looks to me like we are in some kind of windowless cell. It would be great if everyone could introduce themselves and then we can look for a way out of here."

Martin wasted no time, he knew at least part of what was going on. "All right, look folks, I'm military, and I can tell you at least one thing. When I awoke I was still suffering the effects of M Jel. From the looks of you all I'd say you were too. I've been involved in some experiments, so this does not come as a surprise to me, but you three are another story."

"I do feel woozy. But I don't know why I would have been given something like that, I have never even heard of it. By the way my name is Regina." said the woman.

Nicholas looked as though he had had his fair share of experience with drugs. His lips curled up when he heard the name M-Jel mentioned. He had a Squirrely demeanor, causing both Martin and Raymond to eye the man suspiciously. They also eyed each other with caution.

"It looks like there's some stuff around here, let's all have a look. Martin, why don't you check around the edges and see if there is some kind of door or something." said Raymond, taking the lead, and eager to find a way out.

"There's a whole case of M-Jel over here." shouted Nicholas, betraying his knowledge of the substance.

Martin, the military man, came through once again. "That's great news, this stuff is made out of the same crap that they make plastic explosives out of. You just found our ticket out of here, buddy."

Raymond was staggered by this, "You're telling me that the military uses the same substance to blow stuff up that it used to drug us? You people really are twisted."

Martin grimaced as he responded, "I don't make this stuff up, I just work for them. People will try and get high on anything, the military just happened to find out and exploit it. I was a voluntary test subject, I tell you that stuff packs a punch, makes you really susceptible to suggestion."

"Who cares what it's used for if it can get us out of here? I say we just rig it up and blow our way out, unless you feel like staying in captivity." said Nicholas. Regina stood at his side nodding her approval.

"It will take me a while to set this up, I'm going to have to rig up a fuse. Raymond, Nicholas, you guys come over here and help me. Regina, see if you can find the thinnest spot in the wall." Martin had no problem taking charge and was doing a better job of it than Raymond.

The two men joined him in fashioning the bomb and Regina did as ordered, searching the crack along the floor to try and find a weak spot. When she thought she had she pointed it out to Martin who grumbled with approval.

Nicholas and Raymond were next to useless and did little to help Martin aside from arguing with each other. Raymond was a revolutionary, a fighter for social justice, and a member of the anti war party. Nicholas was a narc that worked for the police, turning in drug dealers and what not. To Raymond, Nicholas was worse than the enemy, he would rather side with a military man then a narc, any day. But for some reason both of them made the unspoken decision to not let the others know that they knew each other. They had bad blood in the street, but it was not going to help them get out of this cage.

Martin worked with skill and in not too much time had fashioned a fuse that would work to ignite the plastic explosive M-Jel. The four captives made what little barricade they could from the rest of the boxes and detritus stored in the cell. Martin placed the makeshift bomb at the weak spot Regina had pointed out, then joined the others hiding behind the boxes.

The bomb went off with mighty force, blowing all of the boxes on top of the captives. It was successful in blowing the door of their prison wide open. They stepped out and marveled at the fact that they were standing in what looked like a small office. Still hazy from the M-Jel they all squinted in the sunlight, so much brighter than Martin's flashlight.

"We were inside of a safe? How did we all fit in there?" asked Martin.

"Forget that, we should search this place and find out why we're here," said Raymond.

Nicolas was wasting no time. He had already begun to rifle through the desk drawers in search of something. The others joined him, not finding much of interest but trashing the place in the process. Exiting the door and finding himself in a living room, Raymond spied a short-wave radio transmitter in the corner. This he pointed out to Martin in excitement, for next to it were pages of scribbled code and several check stubs. Both Martin and Regina came to see.

"These codes look like military. And look, some of them match up with these check numbers." Martin pocketed the paperwork as he explained the find to Raymond. "You grab that transmitter, it will come in handy. Now let's get out of here before someone finds us."

Meanwhile, still in the office, Nicolas found the stash of M-Jel in the closet and took the lot. Dangerous stuff, but the street value was high, and he knew the right buyers. The others joined him back in the office, all suggesting that they get out of there. Nicolas agreed and they fled out of the office, through the living room, and out the front door into the decaying suburbs of what could have been any urban-sprawl town.

Regina stopped in the front yard, "Wait. They're going to be looking for the four of us. We should do something to throw them off of our trail, or make it look like there are more of us involved in the break out."

She had a point and they all knew it. Raymond reacted with gut instinct, picked up a rock and hurled it through the office window. "This way maybe they'll think that someone helped us get out." said Raymond, already beginning to run down the street, his pace hampered by the transmitter.

***

Richard arrived back from the store and was shocked by the disarray of his place. It had been ransacked, his safe destroyed, his new manuscript burnt, and worst of all, the M-Jel was missing. At least with the drugs gone he could call the police.

***

The taller of the two police men looked down at Richard with an expression of pure disgust. "You say someone broke in... This safe has been blown from the inside. Are you sure that you didn't do this yourself?"

The Escape

N ote slipped through the bars. Written on toilet paper and sparkling like a C note. I was thinking it would be a one-way ticket, hoping, desperately so. Could be a blue slip. Could be a 1099. Stopped with the daydreaming and got to work trying to read the scrawl.

"It looks like we are missing some information for your account. Until we receive it, you can't send or withdraw funds."

And that's the chorus of my prison song. I saw all that shiny gold, dove for it, and came up gasping with a fortune in rolls of tin foil. Tried to deposit it after sitting on it for a while, and what do you know, they'd been folded in such a way as to be a dead giveaway to any discerning eye. After accepting the agreement, you'll be all set to continue to use prison services, just don't ask. A federal court authorized this *Notice*. You are not being sued. This is not a solicitation from a lawyer. But it's solid advice for someone in your position. It's a battle plan for your longwinded time here. Your rights are affected whether you act or don't act. Please read this *Notice* carefully. You can choose to opt out of the Settlement and receive no payment, and you sure did. Unless you exclude yourself, you are automatically part of the Settlement, and you sure did. If you do nothing, you will not get a payment from this Settlement and you will give up the right to sue, continue to sue, or be part of another lawsuit against the Defendant (yourself) related to the legal claims resolved by this Settlement. You've been had, little peanut. All that money won't pay for nothing, gold, tin, or otherwise. You may ask to appear at the hearing but you do not have to appear, HA. Wouldn't you like that to be true. Go there now to accept what's reserved in your name. A hard sentence, life, if you play your cards right. Not even enough left for you to make a hat. Too late for that anyway. Could have been a gold-plated little plaything, but you wanted high stakes and didn't know how to play with the big boys. Now what choice do you have?

I am more horny than I have been in a very long time, I don't know what is up with me. It must be the damp prison walls. While we know the market has taken a turn, we're hoping if we continually touch base that the guards will look the other way and let us get all slippery. Your funds have been approved, send your postal address, to enable us to dispatch our letter/documents to you. By the grace of God, I had no choice than to do what is lawful and right in the sight of God for eternal life and in the sight of man, for witness of God's mercy and glory upon my life please spit first. I plead that you will not expose or betray this trust and confidence that I am about to repose on you for the mutual benefit of the orphans. They'll end up around here sooner or later and I'll wait deliciously. That's why I'm making this decision. I'm not afraid of death, so I know where I'm going. Better realize this sooner than later, cuz the trip is one way.

Late Sister Dorothy Stang bequeathed a large sum to you in the codicil of her last will and testament, but you've been too busy slouching off to know how to read, so we'll spell it out for you. Minus the kinky parts. I am a very skilled designer with various abilities and can develop anything, but you don't have the gold to spur me into action. You have been compensated with the sum of time in this United

Felony, the payment will be issued but there'll be no time to count it as you relearn how to breathe vacuum. Leading Pharmaceutical companies in the UK have a business proposal that might interest you. So, hold that breath. Get back to me, so I can provide you with more information. No, don't speak, it's a waste of air. The author uses the Bible and gives us a unique take on it through poetry. He takes the reader through topics such as nature, the creator, Jesus, but also oppression. Not that you are oppressed, you did this to yourself. No subject is untouched and although the title of this poem may be a shock it just gives us a highlight of the reality of what terrible things go on in our world because of you. Think that they'll find out? Purchases subject to credit approval. Accrued Reward Points that are not re-deemed will be forfeited and circumcised. Please note that it may take up to 10 days to process your request. But then again, you have time to wait. I am a 22-year-old girl and an orphan. My parents have died. My uncle is threatening to kill me because of my inheritance. If you help me I will give you 20% of the total fund for your help after the fund leaves the country. I assure you that this transaction is 100% risk free. Same old song and dance, sounds like good advice and I'd act now if I wasn't sitting here counting bricks to pass the time. Meanwhile, I didn't forget your past efforts and attempts to assist me in transferring those that failed us. So that you will keep the whole secret about my success I've made sure that you stay put for the time being, because I knew that it was only you who knew how I made the money, so try to keep everything very secret. I hope you understand the reason why this huge burden fell upon you. You call it work, I say keep counting those bricks, you're here to measure time. Do you know the amount of the funds that were kept for you? Keep counting. They can't have infinity cuz they can't afford it. And spaceships are expensive too.

Personally, I have not found family members for a long time. They may have left without a word. I notice that you have been receiving numerous missives from people who claim to have the time coming to you, but I advise that if you're still in communication with any of them stop every communication right now because those people are being investigated. Fraud is fun until that moment. And we ain't at the place with new laws yet. That loud engine won't be secret for long and we must keep it hidden until the great escape.

Make money, not war! Financial Robots is what you need. I will give you pictures and more details as soon as I hear from you. Wish you had saved that dime now, don't you?

The great spellcaster ain't free. After 2 years of loneliness, you might think hope was lost. But the great spellcaster makes us happy again. You can contact him too, but he'll have to know where you hid the scratch, if you were smart enough to do so. All that biding your time, and now this. Keep quiet, we know it's hard for you, but by all means keep quiet. He will be of great help because he is a wonderful man. Sit there inventorying the nothing that you've got and wish your way to all those sexy spells:

A planet all to ourselves

Money spell

Pregnancy spell

Love spell

Cult case spell

Fruit of the Womb

Fibroid

Business Boom

Financial Breakthrough

Get Rich without Rituals

Bad Dreams

Promise and Fail

Something to breathe

Epilepsy

Spiritual Attack

Mental Disorder

Guards asleep

Political Appointment

Visa Approval

Cancer

Safe lift off

Examination Success

Good Luck

And on arrival, all smiling and hat waving, sucked in a hot breath of new place, new sands, new sky.

Greetings, from the illuminati world elite empire. Bringing the poor, the needy and the talented to the limelight of fame, riches and powers, knowledge, business and political connections. This is the right time for you to put all your worries, your health issues, and finance problems to an end by joining the Elite Family of The illuminati! Are you sick, barren or having divorce problems, finding it difficult to get job promotions in your place of work. YES! Then join the Illuminati empire you will get all these numerous benefits and solutions to your problems. Beats the can doesn't it? Recruitment scheme, doubtful. They need people like us, willing to go the extra mile in new places. If you are not serious about joining the Illuminati empire, then you are advised not to contact us at all and leave at once. This is because disloyalty is highly not tolerated here in our organization. Go back to Earth with that animal instinct. Those on the inside ought to know this, but some of you candy boys think you can sit around twirling your hair. Meanwhile we have great plans for planet domination and will need a few bad men to take on the task. Don't share this letter with the guards. Course not. Wouldn't think of it. Stupid enough to botch a job to wind up here, but not so dumb as to not eat this letter and nourish myself with dreams of that great escape from the planet. We'll go together when the time comes, and I'll be really handy since the fuel is distrust.

Solvent

F or ages Franklin Hills had been nothing but a landfill serving the Jackson County area. When the population boomed the land had been speedily re-appropriated by developers, and the area had become a sprawling suburb complete with strip malls, cookie-cutter houses, and golf courses. Families had filled the town quickly, most of them moving there for the new industry growth in chemical solvents. Because of this the Franklin Hills area consisted, at least its adult population, of chemists and engineers. Due to the area having been a landfill prior to the building of the city, houses and parks were only allowed to be built in certain areas. Where the main hill of the landfill had once stood was now a beautiful and sprawling cemetery, complete with a lake and white marble mausoleum.

Dale Gibson pulled his sedan out of his driveway into the wide streets of the neighborhood, it was a short drive up to the chemical plant and he would make it to work on time, but today he dreaded going. Yesterday had been his wife Carolyn's birthday and he had drunk too much champagne at the dinner party they had hosted with some friends. When he woke up this morning his head felt like it had been kicked multiple times. He took two aspirin and threw them up immediately, today was going to be rough.

He wondered if he shouldn't have called in sick today as he slid his I.D. entry card, but Dale had only been working at Bionetics International for a few months and thought that it was probably too soon to be calling in. He donned his lab coat and scurried up to his laboratory. Today he would be finishing the analysis of a new solvent for cleaning heavy duty industrial greases. It was fairly boring work, but he was reaching the end of this particular project and wanted to make a good impression on the boss. His headache raged and he wished that it was lunch time already. Unable to pull himself together for the moment he gazed out the window overlooking the attractive but sinister sight of the local graveyard. The graveyard, along with the lab, had been built within the last few decades, therefore it was only partially filled. Only about a quarter of the plots held graves and they were concentrated in the section below his window.

Dale gathered himself and started filling out some paperwork regarding the tests he was finishing. He was glad that the office supplied coffee, of all days he needed it today. He took a sip of the warm brew and set it down on the lab table before going back to the forms he was filling out. He cursed himself for drinking on a weekday, it was nearly impossible to keep focused. As he poured over the numbers on the paper in front of him he reached for his mug. Unintentionally he picked up a beaker of solvent that sat next to his coffee and began to take a deep swill. As the liquid hit his tongue he knew that he would be sick. Before swallowing he ran to the window and spit the vile fluid out, in his retching he also lost the beaker which he had failed to set down and it went crashing to the floor beneath. How embarrassing, thank god no one else was in the lab that morning, he was too seasoned a professional to be making such mistakes. He ran down to the bathroom to clean himself up, hoping he would not run into anyone on the way, then he would have to go out to the graveyard to collect the remains of the shattered beaker.

The solvent that Dale had been working with was of special new design. The scientists had altered the valence electrons of certain molecules to make them interact with industrial chemicals in a corrosive but gentle manner. It was a triumph of chemistry and electricity combined and would surely revolutionize the solvent market. As Dale washed his mouth out in the restroom the solvent he had dropped out the window began to work its way into the soil upon which it had fallen. The earth that had once been landfill was rich in fertilizers and many other chemicals that were the byproducts of all that trash out-gassing for years. In the decades before Franklin Hills had been developed the environmental protection laws had been slack and many chemicals and other waste had made it into the ground that shouldn't have. Dale's solvent stripped its way through the earth, shaving off electrons as it went and interacted with chemicals that it had never been designed to encounter. Gaining energy as it moved, it picked up speed and began to illuminate as it became a seething ball of liquid electricity devouring electrons in its path. Dale decided that he would have to take the rest of the day off. No matter what impression he wanted to make on his boss, these kinds of mistakes were unacceptable. He cursed himself for his negligence and decided to have lunch on his way home. He had a horrible stomach ache from the little bit of solvent he had swallowed and hoped that food would settle his digestion.

***

The cleaning crew finished tidying up the offices of Bionetics International then started locking up the building. They were always the last to leave and had to follow strict closing procedures due to some of the work that the company was engaged in was for defense companies that needed to remain secret.

Al, the head janitor, hung up his overalls in his locker and made for the main exit, making sure he had his keys to lock the place. Then he set the alarm and set out for his car. He had always found it slightly creepy that the parking lot was butt up against a cemetery, but such was life in Franklin Hills. As he started up his car he wondered if any of his pals would be down and the bar, it was one of those nights. Al's friend Hank had died several weeks ago of an aneurysm, no one had seen it coming and then suddenly he was gone. He had been buried at Franklin Hills, and Al had to walk right by his grave every work day on the way to his car, a constant reminder.

Dale slept off his hangover as Al began working on his next one, Hank also slept but more deeply and quietly. For hours the seething ball of electric fluid had worked its way down into the soil and had grown bigger as it descended. It writhed in electric fashion, a swirling mass of quantum energy, barely contained by its own field. It moved through the newly packed earth until it bumped into something that would be solid to any other entity, Hank's coffin. The glowing ball passed through the wood and sensed the potential in front of it. Hank's brain was only partially decomposed and the ball saw in it a new seat, a place to settle down. The electricity entered through the nose and worked its way into the brain, finding it comfortable, all of the electric pathways already laid out, a place of order, a place it could be more than a loose knit sphere.

For the first time in weeks Hank opened his eyes, but it was no longer Hank, rather his shell driven by something else altogether. His hands jerked up and began clawing at the coffin encompassing him. He felt no panic and knew that it would take a while but that he would escape the box that trapped him. One thing and one thing only was on his mind, hunger. When the ball of electric fluid had entered the mind of the dead man a lot of energy loss was the result, and the cumbersome body expended more and more every second. It was evident to the creature that soon it would need to consume another bioelectric system.

Electrosmooth

"Yeti! Yeti! Yeti!" The children all chanted in unison.

"He's so hairy I'll bet he has to comb his whole body."

"My dad says he belongs in a zoo."

"What a freak."

The children of the playground danced around Ralph, dropping insults and teasing in the sing-song manner of their age. From out of nowhere a stone struck Ralph on the head, sending him to the asphalt. The chanting stopped and the children stood in a circle, no one daring to say who had thrown the rock. When the bell rang they all ran off to class, leaving Ralph where he had fallen. It was the last day that he ever attended school.

***

"Do you suffer from unwanted hair? Are you tired of razors, powders, and creams that don't work? If so, then the new Electrosmooth from Bionetics International is the solution for you. The Electrosmooth zaps unwanted hair out of existence with its new pain-free, patented Quantalaz technology..."

Annoyed, Ralph switched off the television. Did even the TV need to remind him? He walked to the bathroom to look in the mirror and see if he really looked so strange. It was not until he opened the door that he remembered that his mother had removed the mirror. Moping back to the living room, he switched on the T.V. again, his only window to the world of people. Maybe he should buy something like the Electrosmooth.

***

Ducking on his way out the front door, Ralph left his mother's house for the first time in nearly fifteen years. He shielded his eyes to block the harsh light, a light strikingly different from that of the television. In his pocket burned unspent birthday money from years of letters sent by an unmet grandmother. He jogged towards the taxi door while scanning the street, relieved that it was an off hour. The cabby's eyes widened as he asked "where to" through the rearview mirror. All through the drive Ralph caught the stares of more people than he had ever met in person.

***

"You're not going to believe our good luck Eddie. A gold mine just walked into the shop. He looks like some kind of yeti or something, and you guessed it, he's here for an Electrosmooth. Think of the ad campaign it could make. Seems like he doesn't have much dough to me, I'll bet we could even work out a trade offer."

Carson hung up the phone with a feeling of satisfaction. If the boss was pleased then he knew he was onto something.

"Ralph, with your unique gift, and our unique product, we could make quite a team. Why not sign up with us, we'll throw in a free Electrosmooth, and even get you some medical help if it's needed. We think that you'd make a perfect example of how our product can help people, people like yourself." Carson bit his lip in anticipation, knowing that he had Ralph hooked, and that his ad campaign would be a smash success.

***

The lights of the studio dazzled him. Never in his life had he met so many people, and never in his life had he felt so accepted and liked. The people were wonderful, but the best thing of all was that he was going to be on television. Just a commercial, but to Ralph it was the real world, one in which he could finally participate. Behind the scenes was a shock that he was not prepared for, but he resigned to not let it show. He enjoyed the limelight.

***

On his way home he stopped at the store and bought a mirror for the bathroom. For the first time in his life he felt unafraid of the outside world, the one which his mother had demonized since almost before he could remember. Hanging the mirror with pride, he took the first good look at his now hairless face and body. It was foreign and would take getting used to, but he was unashamed.

The telephone interrupted his first prideful moment, but he answered with enthusiasm, wanting to talk to someone. The voice on the other end sounded nervous and excited.

"Ralph, I'm glad you answered. This is Dr. Charleston. It's a miracle that we've found you. You know that we've been trying to track you down ever since you were taken out of school. You're quite a hard man to find. Forgive me for being blunt, but your condition, I mean we've been needing someone with your condition, you see we've discovered that your abnormal hair growth holds the cure for cancer. With one of your hairs we can cross reference genes and destabilize the rapid growth process. It's just that your condition is exceedingly rare, and you are believed to be the last hypertrichiac alive. With your help we could save thousands of lives."

In the mirror Ralph watched as his smile sagged. The phone sank back into the cradle. In front of him sat the box that housed the Electrosmooth. Bold letters on the side of the box read, results permanent.

Fucking Like Animals

"You'll have to wait in the hallway for a few minutes, I've got some business to finish up here with an associate. Better yet, go get us a cup of coffee and come back in twenty minutes, I should be ready for you then." said Derek dismissively, closing the door on Danny's face.

Danny had no choice but to walk down the street for the coffee. You couldn't argue with someone who was in Derek's line of work. Dealers always had to be in control, always acting like their business was more important than it is. Danny didn't mind, the clubs wouldn't be opening for hours, he was planning ahead, really wanting the night to go his way, and knowing that the pills took a few hours to kick in. He grabbed two cups of old coffee at the donut store, poured copious amounts of sugar into them, and started back for Derek's apartment.

"OK come on in, Danny." Derek barked through the intercom.

Multiple deadbolts rattled before Danny was let into the dark apartment. One of those places where you can't tell what time it is because the room has never seen the light of day, at least not with its current occupant. He strolled in and sat on the couch, taking the bong that Derek handed him and inhaling a huge hit from the water pipe. Smoke trailed from Danny's mouth as his eyes grew visibly redder and his voice deepened half an octave. They both lit cigarettes and sat smoking in silence, pretending to be friends, but really having nothing to say. When the obligatory courtesies were over Danny nervously breached the subject.

"Do you have any more of that *Bird* stuff? You weren't kidding about that shit, it really got me going." Danny asked enthusiastically, his tone back to normal.

"What did I tell you? I always have the best and newest stuff. I don't have the same shit as last time but I've got a different strain of *Bird* that I know you'll dig." said Derek dismissing Danny's comment and rifling through a wooden box that he kept under his recliner chair.

Danny watched as smoke curled to the ceiling, knowing that Derek did not like to be interrupted while exploring his stash. "Last time I saw you I went to Club Intra, and man, that shit really worked like you said it would. I was out there cutting-a-rug like never before, and just like you said, the girls sure did notice. I had a fucking circle of people around me watching me dance, can you believe it, the Friday before last, no one even noticed I was alive and out there on the dance floor."

"Of course you were, like I said I have the best *Bird* in town. Here's the new strain, made from some jungle variety. You know, it's the ones you've never heard of that have the craziest effects. Probably seen it on the nature channel or something, they use it the same way we do, works for them too." said Derek while waving the small baggy in Danny's direction.

Danny grabbed the bag, putting on his least threatening air, trying not to agitate the high-strung dealer. "Is this one going to have the same effects? I mean, I really liked that last stuff, and I'm hoping for a similar experience. Sure you don't have any more of that last shit?"

"Ran out shortly after I saw you last. Don't worry, you're gonna flip when you try this. From what I understand this variety will have you dancing even harder, and they'll notice, I guarantee it." Derek held out his hand as he spoke. His way of saying that a conversation was over and it was time to pay up and leave. There were probably a few people waiting out in the hallway as Danny had before.

He handed over the money and took the baggie, slapped Derek a high-five and hit the street, still with several hours to go before he could show up fashionably late at Club Intra.

***

"You feel like going out with me tonight, darling? I'm going to the club to meet up with some of the girls, you're welcome to join us if you like." asked Clara.

"I wish I could, but you already know that I'm on graveyard shift again tonight. While you'll be having drinks, I'll be packing boxes. You have fun, cutie. We'll just have to catch up in the morning. I have to leave after this cup of coffee, do you want a glass of wine before you're off too." replied Frank.

"Yes please." shouted Clara from the bathroom as she flat-ironed her hair and primed for her night out. Secretly she was glad that Frank had to work. He wasn't as much fun as he used to be before he had taken his new job. He was always tired now, and rarely felt like dancing, always complaining that her night was his morning, and who would want to dance first thing in the morning?

He set the glass of wine on the bathroom counter and ran his fingers through her still warm hair, gave her a peck on the cheek so as not to smear her newly applied lipstick, and patted her on the ass, then left for work worrying that he would be late.

A wave of relief flooded over Clara as she heard his car speed up the driveway and out into the street. She would have the whole night without him and planned to cut loose. She'd been tied up in the house too long, and if he wasn't going to go out to the clubs it wouldn't stop her from having a good time. She took a Xanax from her purse and washed it down with the wine, draining the glass with one swing, then slid to the kitchen for a refill. She was going to start this night relaxed and feeling good.

***

The line to get into Club Intra went all the way around the block. Seas of dolled up girls and drooling guys smoked endless waves of cigarettes as they waited and prayed to get in. Clara met with her friends Janet and Sarah in the parking lot and passed a bottle around in the car, getting their buzz on, and saving money at the bar. Not that any of them would have to pay for their drinks once they got inside. After drinking for half an hour and killing a pint of vodka they made their way to the line.

"Hey! You, three ladies over there. You can come to the front of the line." shouted the bouncer. It wasn't the first time that the girls had been flagged from the line and allowed to get in without waiting. One of the perks of being sexy females.

***

The girls' luck wasn't as good with the line at the bar. They fell into their place and waited while people-watching and chatting it up. Several times Janet pointed out guys in the crowd that caught her eye, she was always on the prowl. When one particularly hot guy walked by she couldn't contain herself any longer, "A girl ought to be able to get lucky at a place like this, Intra is always crawling with fresh blood." The girls all laughed and hooted at the guy that had walked by, their voices fading into the loud music and crowd noise.

When they were half way through the line Sarah pulled out a small baggie containing three pink pills with brown flecks, "You guys want to try some *Cat*, it's the latest thing on the street, just picked it up from a friend, says not too many people have even heard of it yet. It's supposed to get you going real good, like *Molly* but better."

Without further conversation the girls divvied up the pills, not waiting for their drinks to wash them down, swallowing them dry. Just then they caught the bartender's eye and the vodka continued to flow. They staked out a table on the edge of the dance floor, sitting with their drinks and waiting for the *Cat* to kick in, while eyeing prospective men and making fun of those with less than graceful dance moves.

The drinks were already working, and the new sensation of *Cat* also began to pulse through their bodies, perking their minds. The feeling was sharp and came on like needles all over the body, or like the sick thrill of a leg filled with sleep coming back to life.

"I feel sleek." Clara was the first to announce the head change.

"Predatory." followed Janet.

"I told you that you guys would love this shit. Wait until it kicks in full force, we're gonna be slinking around that dance floor like we never have before." said Sarah proudly. She always took pride in having the latest thing in her pocket, always hungry for new experience and someone to share it with.

When Clara got up to go to the bathroom she realized that her movements were different. Each step that she took was more like a leap. She glided through the crowd with an accuracy that she had never known, sliding right through the gaps between dancers, never rubbing shoulders. As her body curved, she had the fleeting epiphany that she must look good from across the room. She was slicker than ever. Sexy.

Arriving back at the table she could see by the look on her friend's face that the drug was kicking in for her too. Janet had already made her way to the floor and was rubbing up against the hottie that had passed them at the bar. In the flashing lights Clara could tell that he was not as cute as they had thought in the dim light, but Janet didn't seem to mind and was getting pretty fresh in a hurry.

"You wanna go dance too, looks like fun?" asked Sarah.

Clara was eager, but not quite ready, "Let's have one more drink and then join her, I feel like getting fucked up tonight."

The waiter plopped two more vodka tonics in front of them and asked about their tab before leaving them alone again. The girls sipped on the drinks and chatted about love-life problems for a minute before deciding to switch the topic of conversation to something more light-hearted and fun. As Sarah was telling her about a new Joe she had met, Clara noticed a guy out on the dance floor, not far off from where Janet was still dancing.

The man was dancing with wild abandon, moving like nothing she had ever seen. He looked so loose, like he was really enjoying himself no matter what was going on around him. Clara wanted to be that free too, she couldn't remember the last time she had had a good time the way that the dancing fellow was. His moves were so alluring, like they were designed to draw one in, they had a hypnotic suggestion to them and they were working their magic on her. She had the sudden and irresistible need to pounce on the dancer, to encompass him. Now she understood the "predatory" comment that Janet had made, it was coming on strong.

She looked to Sarah and announced, "See that dancing fool over there, he's got a thing. I'm gonna go dance with him, would you mind checking in my coat with yours?" Without waiting for a reply she downed the last of her vodka tonic and made her way across the dance floor to the guy that had caught her attention.

He moved wildly, arms and legs flowing in such a way that it hardly looked human, but still with an appealing and odd grace to the movements. He knew the moonwalk, not to mention a score of other moves that were not in the book. He seemed tireless and energetic, even the sweat on his brow had some kind of natural allure. Clara's back arched as she approached him, and decided not to say anything but just to join in the dance.

She almost had a difficult time keeping up with him, but the *Cat* pulsing through her kept her vibrant and alert. She mirrored some of his moves, surprised that she had such abilities at dance. When she fell short he guided her, twirling her with such speed that it made her giddy and elated. They danced through endless songs, she forgetting all about the friends she had come with, and he focusing all of his attention on her. Clara didn't care what music was playing. She was centered on him, without even knowing his name. He was like prey in the crosshairs of her mind. Images of pouncing him flooded her thoughts.

Drenched with sweat he asked her if she would like to grab another drink at the bar. "Why don't we leave instead?" she suggested, the images still running through her.

His smile said an eager yes as he shouted over the music, "By the way, my name is Danny, what's yours?"

Clara forgot all about the coat check as they headed for the door.

***

Clara rode Danny with the ferocity of a woman pent up, climbing on top of him and with every nerve of her body trying to rock his world in a way he had never known.

"Hey slow down a little bit, I want to enjoy it." breathed Danny heavily.

Danny displayed none of the prowess that he had on the dance floor. Still she didn't slow down and he came in three anti-climactic spurts, the whole event being over in several fleeting moments. He rolled over and passed out whispering something about *Bird* that she couldn't have understood even if she had been paying attention.

Fuck. That was hardly worth it. Didn't even get to toy with him. I can't believe I just cheated on Frank for that lousy lay. He didn't even seem to like me that much, just fell right asleep. At least this was the only time. I mean, last time didn't count cuz it was only drunken kissing. And the other thing... This time I really took it there, it must be the drugs. That's it, it was the drugs.

***

"Cutie, I'm home. I've got a treat for you." announced Frank on his way into the apartment. His cry was met by silence. The house was empty.

She must have gotten drunk and is staying with one of the girls. I hope they weren't drunk driving all night. She must be safe. I'll let her sleep it off then give her a call.

Frank got ready for bed as the rest of the world was waking, had his morning glass of wine then went to sleep trying to drown out the hustle and bustle of the now awake city with pleasant thoughts.

When he awoke the bed was still empty. Disturbed, he crawled into the shower to get ready for another long night of toiling away with shipping and receiving. He dressed himself and was about to run out the door when Clara arrived, make-up smeared face, and reeking like alcohol.

"Fun night huh, cutie? Looks like you really got into it. Where'd you stay last night, I was starting to get worried about you. And where's the coat that I gave you, you were wearing it last night?" questioned Frank.

"I stayed out at Janet's place. They were way too drunk to drive me home, I think I left my jacket in Sarah's car. We had a great time at Intra. So many new people show up there all of the time. You should really come with us sometime." said Clara casually.

"Yeah, if I ever get a night off! I gotta run off to work now. You look like you could use a little rest, I'll see you in the morning, OK." Grabbing his bag he headed out the door to his old beater.

***

"Look, Derek, this stuff worked great on the dance floor, but it made me a two-pump-chump. What the hell?" said Danny.

"Maybe you just aren't getting enough." replied Derek with his particular brand of condescension.

"The *Bird* you gave me last time was a scam, what good is getting the girls if you can't enjoy them afterwards?"

"OK, Danny, I've got what you need. You just let Doctor Derek fix you up. You know I've got a solution for everything. Wait until you hear what I've got up my sleeve."

"If it's more of that last *Bird* you had I don't want it, that shit caused me problems. I'll bet it's the last time I score with this chick I met, as she was smokin'!" interrupted Danny.

"Just let me finish, son. You still want the *Bird*, I guarantee it. But this time you gotta try *Rat* with it. Ever hear of those rodents, or marsupials, or whatever they are, that fuck for weeks straight? Well you're gonna screw like one of them if you take this stuff. You can take it with the *Bird*, use you're dancing to lure em in, then finish the job with this stuff." Derek beamed with showy confidence as he took out two small baggies for Danny to try. "The *Rat* is on me, let me know how it works out, I've had nothing but good reports."

Danny took the bags and handed over his money. Derek didn't usually mess around, so he figured that what he said would go. He'd find out this Friday at any rate.

***

Clara hung up the phone after a brief conversation with Sarah that ended with promises of more *Cat*.

"We're going to Infra again, darling, you gotta work?"

"Yep, you know that. You guys are going there again, don't you ever get enough of that place?" replied Frank.

"I like the music they play there, and the drinks are reasonable. I'll probably be here until after you leave, Janet is picking me up and you know how she is always way late. Would you like me to make you some breakfast before you head out to work?" The last bit with a tinge of resentment, she was sick of catering to him. She rarely even got to see him and he was always so tired that he stayed in a perpetual condition of acting short with her.

"No thanks, cutie, I'll pick up something on the way to work. You have fun with the girls, try not to stay out so late this time so I can actually hang out with you between shifts." And he was gone again, leaving her in the empty apartment with nothing to do but wait and get into the wine early.

***

"Hey, Clara, isn't that the guy you went home with last time we were here?" asked Janet. Clara hesitated before stuttering, "Uh, yeah, I think so, it's kinda blurry to me."

"Well that guy sure can dance, look at him out there, I'll bet he was good in bed too..." joined Sarah.

"Not really, anyway, shut up about it, and keep quiet around Frank. The real highlight of last week was the *Cat*. I've been dying to get into some more, you'll have to introduce me to the guy you get it from." Clara grinned impatiently. "I'll go get us some drinks." She stood up and headed for the bar, eager for the sleekness of *Cat*.

"Can I get those drinks for you, baby?" A bold stranger stood next to her at the bar, money in hand, leg beating to the music.

"Thanks, buddy!" called out Clara as she gripped the three glasses in her hands and walked away from the stranger before he could ask another question. She was getting good at this, and the *Cat* wasn't even inside of her yet. The evening was going to flow.

She set down the drinks in front of the girls and Sarah handed her a pill. "Bottoms up." Three glasses slammed down on the table simultaneously, the night was about to begin. Clara opened her purse and pulled out a compact to check her face. The inside of her purse was illuminated by the blue light of her cell. She pulled out the phone and checked the texts.

<Have fun, angel. Hopefully I'll be off work by six thirty, if I'm lucky they might even let me go early. Kiss>

What timing. It's like he knows and wants me to feel guilty for having a good time. Just because he's a stick in the mud doesn't mean that I can't party and have a good time. He's so boring he probably wouldn't even give Cat *a try. He belongs at work.*

Clara put aside these thoughts and went back to focusing on having a good time. As usual Janet was already on the dance floor, not even waiting for the *Cat* to kick in.

Sarah spoke first. "How are you and Frank doing? I mean, Brian and I aren't getting on so well. I just can't understand it, he's always eaten with jealousy. It's like he wished he could be as cool as me or something..."

Clara nodded and said yeah at all the appropriate times, but heard none of it. The sleekness had returned and her eyes fixed on Danny across the room. He was spinning like a top, alive and on fire. A group of girls danced, cooing next to him. Brow wet with perspiration he glistened like fresh bait waiting to be hooked. She felt a sudden surge of predatory rage at the sight of the other girls. No one was going to beat her out on this one.

She slid across the floor and cut between the girls and Danny. He didn't notice her right away, lost in the trance of dancing. He opened his eyes as Clara brushed up against him, making sure to put a bit of hip into it. She had his attention now.

She seems so much bigger than before, as if I'm looking at her from below. It must be the drugs. This cocktail has me flying. Derek wasn't kidding about the mix,

A circle cleared around them as they danced. They moved like animals, dripping and ferocious. Others were clearly amused and envious of the grace they were displaying, dancing as if they were years away from being strangers. The music beat them into a frenzy, arms, legs, and hips moving with such speed that the music was almost too slow to keep up with them. Clara lifted a leg and wrapped it around Danny's waist pulling him closer. She needed to devour him, not sure if she could even wait until they were out of the club.

This Cat *is stronger than the last batch. I still can't believe that I can move this way. And he is such a good dancer, last time wasn't a fluke.*

Clara briefly caught the sight of her friends, now both sitting at the table. Both had looks of amazement and envy on their faces sweaty from dancing. They egged her on with a few lewd gestures, gave the signal that meant 'do you want another drink' and at the shake of her head went back to scanning the room for guys of their own. She didn't need any more liquor for now, she was drunk on life, and *Cat*. And she had found her mouse.

Danny's legs were like jelly. Glancing at his watch he realized that he had been on the dance floor without a break for hours. He still felt fresh, but sweat was pouring down his chest, the same chest that concealed his rapid heartbeat. An irresistible desire to make savage love to Clara took over his senses, but she didn't look finished dancing.

I wonder how much longer I can hold out and still have stamina for her. She was a wild one last week.

"I'll be right back." Clara whispered in his ear. She made off towards the table where Sarah and Janet sat talking.

"Looks like you got yourself a catch again." said Janet with a touch of jealousy.

Clara ignored the comment and looked to Sarah, "Do you have any more *Cat*, I really want to take it there, tonight's my night."

Sarah looked slightly disappointed, "Yeah, I've got one left, I was planning on taking tomorrow. I guess if you can pay me back for it right now I'd be willing to part with it."

Without hesitation Clara pulled out her wallet and made the exchange. Moving slower than she had on the dance floor made her realize how sweaty and wet she was, and she headed towards the bathroom to rinse off and wash down another dose of *Cat*.

She emerged from the bathroom after several minutes and spread her gaze around the floor looking for Danny. Her eyes fixed on several cute guys as she scanned the crowd, possibly other prospects for later. From every angle men stared at her, desire beaming and indiscriminate. She had that air about her tonight. Something about the *Cat* stirred something inside of you, and men had no problem noticing.

Where is that guy?

As Clara considered her options Danny emerged from the crowd to her left. The place was packed and it was no wonder that she hadn't noticed him. But her mind was fixed on one thing and one thing only, herself. When she saw him her senses lit up and the predatory feeling rose again into her belly with incomprehensible force. She forgot all about the other guys in the club and slinked towards him, sliding between bodies as if they weren't there at all, as if only the two of them existed, in separate worlds, but with the intimate relationship that only prey and perpetrator can share.

There she is, I'd thought I'd lost her. His heart thumped against his chest in quick short bursts

Their bodies came together again, bare skin slipping, clothes cling-
ing to their moisture. The circle opened for them. Bass rumbled
through the floor, rhythm moved their legs. Their arms found their
way to each other. Dancing was beginning to not be enough.

***

"Do you want a drink?" slurred Danny.

"Got any vodka?" the slurring continued.

"Yeah, what do you want for a mixer?"

"Straight's fine."

Clara went to the bathroom to splash water on her face as the drinks
were being poured. *It's damn hot in here. It's gonna make me sick.*
Staggering to the toilet there was no time to raise the seat. Vomit
sprayed the lid and the surrounding wall. Splashing water on her face
she gathered herself enough to find a washcloth and clean the muck.
Damn it Clara this is your moment, get it together. Without rinsing her
mouth she strode towards the living room where Danny waited with
the drinks. She half fell towards the couch and into his lap as French
disco pop teased her ringing ears.

She watched Danny's mouth move while he spoke, but didn't take
in a word. She didn't care what he had to say, she wanted only one
thing. Sip after sip of the vodka cooled her back down and made her
body settle into the couch where she lay. *Why hurry.* She didn't owe
this guy anything, but she was going to have her fun. Leaning over to
kiss him she spilled a bit of her drink on his lap. "So sorry." she half
mused while running her hand over the wet spot in his crotch. He rose
under her touch as she noticed that the skin on his face glistened and
flushed bronze.

Clara bit at his ear while whispering for another drink. *She's toying with me.* Danny stood up and walked awkwardly to the kitchen. His gait betrayed his arousal.

"Mind if I put on another record?" Clara asked half-heartedly as she pushed play on the CD she had already selected. Notes poured out of the speakers and into her throbbing senses. *Frank would hate this music.* But she was loving it, letting it flow through her, almost forgetting about Danny all together. Until he returned with the drink. Throwing back her head she gulped at the vodka, drinking with an air of authority, wanting to look like a pro in the overly eager man's eyes. He seemed nervous and leaning her head on his chest she could feel the rapid beating of his heart.

While she wasn't looking Danny slipped another *Rat* into his mouth and swallowed hard. *I'm not risking blowing this.* Clara didn't notice or she might have asked to try one too. Instead she loosened his belt and slid it off of his pants. He lifted himself slightly from the couch, allowing her to do so. When the belt hung limp in her hand she slapped his thigh with it.

"Ahhhh!" surprise got the best of him. Before he could speak she clawed at his neck, pulling him into her and joining their lips. He rose again and reached for her breast.

With speed and accuracy she didn't know she had slapped his hand away. "Easy girl..." Danny slurred.

Clara put her hand to his lips and stopped his words with a finger in his mouth. With her other hand she teased him through his pants. She straddled him and bit at his neck before pulling him onto the floor. He fell on top of her and moved in for a kiss. This she avoided and rolled to position herself on top of him once more. Buttons popped and flew in every direction as she tore his shirt out of her way. His chest also showed bronze. Clara ran her tongue across it, tasting the salt of his perspiration.

It was obvious that Danny wanted to switch positions and bend Clara over the couch, but she didn't give him the opportunity. She pulled his pants down just enough to reveal his equipment. Not wanting to waste time on undressing she hiked her skirt and pulled her panties aside, forgetting all about the rubbers in her purse. And she rode.

She moved like she was alone. Screwing so openly that she might have well been by herself masturbating. He had more in him this time and she was going to take advantage. Then she noticed him. *Uh, his face looks bloated. And so sweaty. Is that normal?*

Danny felt tremors in his arms, legs and back and mistook them for a precursor to orgasm. *Hold on champ, you're doing better than last time.* His heart pounded, he thought he might faint. So awake but drowsy at the same time. For a moment he forgot what was going on. Then his confusion focused into an acute headache. *Get it together, man. Got to enjoy this while you can.* Danny was wishing he had avoided that last drink. Incredible thirst overtook him. The room seemed too hot. *Just hold on a minute. Almost there.*

Blue light seared behind Danny's eyes and he ejaculated in one final thrust and fell limp. Clara felt the hot outpour flood inside of her. *Did he just cum in me? Crap!* She leapt up from his crotch. "What are you thinking?!" she demanded.

He responded with silence. Already losing the heat that his body had been exuding. She repeated herself, and again silence. Purple streaks rose from his skin all over his body and his face seemed even more swollen than before. *This isn't good.* She struggled for her purse and grabbed her phone. Another text.

<You OK, baby? It's late and I haven't heard from you yet.>

What timing. She ignored the text and dialed.

"911 emergency."

In between deep gasps she managed to say, "I need an ambulance right away. A heart attack, or an OD or something."

The next minutes disappeared into a flood of despairing thought. When she finally looked up, an EMT was repeating his question to her, "What have you guys been taking tonight?"

His tone induced her into a new state of semi-clarity. "I don't know about him, but I was taking *Cat*. And we were both drinking heavily." Lying wasn't going to do any good here.

"You kids and these animal hormones, who in the world would think that taking that stuff was a good idea. Jim, we've got another endocrine failure on our hands. I think we lost him already, but try a shot of adrenaline. And we should be taking you in too, that stuff is dangerous."

"If I have a choice I'll just be on my way. I don't even know this guy." Clara texted for a cab while speaking.

***

Clara hung up the phone with the doctor and immediately called Sarah, "You remember a few months ago when I left with that guy? How I told you he came in me when he died?"

"Yeah, you poor thing. It's so horrible I can't believe it." Sarah had already heard the story a few times and knew that Clara was having a hard time digesting all of it.

"I just got off the phone with the clinic. It's so much worse than I thought. I missed my period so I went in for a pregnancy test and..."

Sarah interrupted, "Oh no! You're pregnant?! What are you going to do?"

"It's worse than that. The doctor said that it's some kind of fluke. He said I make Octomom look normal. I'm pregnant with ten babies. He called it a litter. And said that my body couldn't possibly handle the stress. I'm going to have to abort." Her voice was choking up and the words came between increasing sobs.

"Oh my God, girl. It's terrible. Don't worry I'll be there for you. Whatever you do, just don't tell Frank. You don't need that making this mess worse. Do you want me to come over?" Her question was returned with sobbing.

Sarah hung up the phone and dialed Janet.

Welcome Home

S ara spat, hitting her target on the battle scarred perspex. "What you're doing is evil!" she shouted while waving a placard with the same sentiment.

The soldiers marched on, their parade anything but triumphant. The one she'd hit didn't bat an eye, didn't even glance her way. His gaze looked past the crowd, billions of miles away, devoid of recognizable emotion.

"Shame on you. Life is precious, all life, even alien life." She kept screaming even though there was no response. Many others in the crowd shouted insults as well, but most gave her dirty looks when they realized what she was saying. Letting the placard fall to the ground she stomped her way out of the throng. This approach was getting nowhere.

She locked eyes with several of those in the crowd and gave the signal. Plan B. They would reconvene in the nearby building staked out before the parade.

***

"We'll have to move quickly. We should have known that peaceful protest wouldn't get anyone's meaningful attention. Everybody, move. We don't have long to pull this off."

Heads nodded all around the group. They looked scared. How could they not? Each and every one of them had sworn to go through with it, but none had truly engaged in violence before. Each moved in their separate directions, a choreography of dissent. Sara patted each on the back as they left. "You got this. You know what to do."

***

The troops all convened in the square. Silent and austere they didn't respond to the flowers being thrown or the cries of thanks from the people gathered. They didn't even speak amongst themselves. This parade was merely a morale booster for the folks they had been protecting, another duty for the tired veterans.

Sara scanned the soldiers with binoculars from the roof of a nearby building. She sensed coldness permeating through the men and women in uniform. *Murderers*, she thought. It would only be minutes now and the gathered crowd would get a taste of what had really been happening so far from home.

***

In the middle of the group the soldier wiped his faceplate while shaking his head. As if he hadn't been through enough already, seen every abomination possible, human and otherwise. Now the people he had risked his life to protect were filled with the same hatred as the enemy.

A battle-sister slapped him on the back. "Shake it off, buddy. These people don't know shit."

He nodded slowly. He understood the anger but had been through enough already. More than anyone should have to go through. All of them had.

***

Below the street Sara's ramshackle gang set the timer on the explosives. If they had set everything up right the blast should blow the manhole and cut right through the gathered soldiers. *Bring the war home.* That was the idea, anyway.

"I hope we're doing the right thing. I mean, those are people too."

"They're monsters and you know it. It's too late to back out now. Let's go." They retreated through the tunnels, hoping to get a safe distance before the action started. Sara spoke into her walkie, "Are we all set. They'll be moving again soon. Two minutes max."

A moment later the reply came from within the tunnels, "Timer set and counting. Right on schedule."

***

Flowers and confetti still rained down on the soldiers.

"Thank God there's no fireworks."

"I think they warned the people ahead of time. I mean, about the fireworks. I'm sure they don't understand why."

"Still, this trash flying through the air is giving me the jitters. Too close to..."

A blast from the brass band cut off the conversation, and several of the soldiers ducked in conditioned fear. They had been ordered to stand tall, but the crowd and the music was too much. Hectic like the battlefield.

Sara watched the commotion, focusing in on the soldier whose faceplate she had soiled. The name patch above the pocket came into view. Private Peters. Panning up to his face she could see the tears streaming down his cheeks.

Oh God, what are we doing? She reached for the walkie again and screamed into it, "Stop! Call off the attack. We can't do this to..."

Her shouting was drowned out, a crack broke through the sky, and another from below. Severed limbs and helmets spattered through the air above the crowds. Screams accompanied the chaos. People ran in all directions, those who could still run. The carnage was thick. But the screeching from above didn't stop.

Sara looked down at the wreckage of what had once been the troops. Guilt shattered her soul. And the firing continued. Blue streaks came from above and tore through the remaining crowd. Vehicles and bodies came apart.

Looking up she understood why the sounds of bombs had not stopped. The alien enemy was here.

Disophonia

The noise almost never stopped. Constant distraction. No matter where Frank went it followed. And then there was silence. It replaced the sound of the engines, finally something to interfere. For a moment a blissful rising inside of him, a rush of beauty that was so unlike the cacophony that generally sounded him that it almost went unnoticed. In fact, he didn't notice the sound of the engines die off, it was the silence in his mind that struck first. Pleasant at first, a rare beauty, foreign.

Words. Words had filled his mind for the entire trip. Now, nothing. The absence crept up before he knew that the words were gone from him. He spoke several out loud to see if they had gone entirely, they came out as mush. If there was someone else to speak to he would have tested the mush to see if it was understandable, but alone, alone, alone. It was probably why the words had stopped. He rarely spoke aloud, there was no reason to, unless he felt the need to keep himself company in the loneliness of the trip. He figured it was why his mind was always reeling, always speaking to himself internally. But now the silence.

So what if the words were gone, the silence was welcome. But where was the sound of the engines? Whenever he stopped his internal mumbling, theirs would take over, like the gentle lull of a cat's purr, always there to accompany him whether welcome or not. The music of the ship he had called it. And he wasn't a fan of music. Something he had had to convince himself was not true, frequently reminding himself that everything had its rhythm, its tone, frequencies, phase cancellations, and all that. A mess really. But where had they gone? Welcome change or not, the ship should be noisy.

He sniffed. An electrical problem? Fire? He smelled nothing. The ship was as vacant of scent as it was sound. Was the lack of stimuli emanating from him? How could nothing emanate at all? Pinching himself he found that his tactile senses remained. He could feel. Everything looked to be in order. For a moment he feared that the oxygen had somehow been vented, but he had no trouble breathing. It had not grown cold either. But that silence. It was as if the void had entered the ship and accompanied him in the cabin.

Again he spoke, but no sound reached his ears, nor did the internal mumble reach him from within. The sensation was not unlike being underwater, cut off from the visible world around him. It was tempting to test the silence with music from the speakers, but he had brought none. The silence of space was one of the appealing parts of the trip, but that was before sound had stopped altogether. The absence would have brought panic but there were no words inside to express the feeling. Nothing.

Was there a hull breach bringing on the early effects of hypoxia? His cognitive ability didn't seem impaired. At least he didn't think so. On to system checks then. While the problem might not be an easy fix, identifying if there was a problem at all should be standard procedure. He went about it. Nothing. As deep a nothing as that which kept his mind silent through what should have been horror.

<I'm losing my mind?> the words were mouthed, but again, nothing but the movement of his face.

He froze. The system checks had revealed nothing. He strained to listen. Nothing. Not even the sound of his own heartbeat. The silence was total. It was thick and unnerving. Taking a different approach he drummed on the console. Nothing. He fingered his ear. Nothing. He roared against the silence. Nothing. No way to express the feelings that accompanied his predicament.

Internal dialog has ceased. Akin to some forms of enlightenment he had heard of, but the terror that this silence brought did not speak to any form of wellbeing, or peace. He checked the lavatory mirror to make sure that he was still there. It revealed nothing new, merely the same image he saw every time he visited the john. He thought to make a call to mission control, but the time lag would stifle any possible comfort it might bring. He did it anyway, to see if the playback might bring his voice back to life. The FFT flatlined in front of him. He could see the silence like an EEG announcing the death of a loved one.

The void had entered him. More nothingness than imaginable. He had to know why. Had to know why even amidst his non-terror that terror spoke so softly as to be silent. The void knew. It must. And if the void had entered him did it still permeate the outside. Was the empty loneliness of space still omnipresent on the other side of the ship's thin walls. There was only one way to know for sure. Floating past his unoccupied space suit he moved to the airlock, punched in the command to vent the cabin, and entered the void straining to hear the music of the cosmos.

Birth of Fire

A great blackness abounds. Aside from the density the blackness is all that exists, a seething foam of potential. The state is timeless, cold, thoughtless, peaceful temporarily. Yet, the dust needs to settle. Once agitated, it begins to move, coalescing towards itself. A pocket here, a pocket there, quickly then slowly, creating time as it goes. Thirteen billion years later he offers her a ride home from work. He's been waiting for the opportunity and stayed late just for this reason. Great accreting discs form in the blackness. The building blocks of mass begin to find each other. Forces separate. The darkness grows without reference point or observer. She accepts. He grins. Why go straight home? Small bubbles of warmth fall inward becoming heat. The swirling mass finds shape here and there as here and there become places in the darkness. The density steps outward, dissipating, rarefying in some places, condensing in others. She gets in the car. He suggests a drink. She accepts. Motion in the blackness. Spinning, all things spin, moving in the nothingness. Hydrogen forms, clumps, finds its kin.

Another man waits on their porch. Awaits her return. He too drinks, looking at the night sky, contemplating its blackness and its fire. The darkness engulfs him. The city lights have swallowed the stars. They are disconnected from the cosmos. Matter joins matter in a timeless dance that makes time in its wake. Hydrogen heats up. A small glow at first, growing hotter in Planck units. As the first things find each other the fabric of creation erupts from the void. The forces work upon each other. She and the suitor arrive at the bar. Drinks are poured. The ceiling blocks the few stars that are left. He buys her a drink, no, she offers to pay. Preferring to feel in control of her indulgences. The waiting man cries out to the stars. He feels that infinite blackness around him. He knows that light is nothing without the information that observers provide. He follows the light back to the beginning - yearning for creation. She laughs at the suitor's jokes. He flatters her. She sees them in the mirror behind the bar and searches his face for that familiar look of longing. She finds it there, drinks deeply, and wonders if it is for her alone.

On the porch the stars come alive. He is near the beginning of time. Sees the ignition. The heavens burn with the first light, the first real information. Witnessing this event terrifies him. From darkness to light the transition burns his eyes. Tears do little to extinguish the searing light. The spinning clock of the stars tells him that it has become late. She has not arrived or announced the tardiness. Planets rise and fall, always heading west toward the infinite sea of space. Last call. They order again. The suitor insists on paying this time, wanting for a good impression and further contact. In his mind he has been laboring for this date. Desires another, and more. Buzzed and jovial they drink until closing time. The lights in the bar go out. The lights of the universe flicker. They begin to shine. On the porch waiting he sees back through billions of years. Light flowing forever, measuring vast distances, shifting in the expansion. Generations of stars dying and giving birth. They get in the car and move swiftly, drunkenly, through the city streets. Relative positions shift. The suitor puts his hand on her thigh. She makes no move to arrest his palm. Nervous sweat soaks into tights. In the side view mirror she sees her smile reflected back to her. The city lights have stolen the stars.

On the porch he waits in frozen limbo. Cars pass in the night like comets. He hopes that each brings her smiling face. The hours tick away. What's left of the stars spin. In the passenger seat she looks up from the mirror to see his worried face gazing out from the porch steps. She looks to her lap and sees the suitor's hand, still attached and wanting. To be needed from two places at once. She smiles. Suggests a spot down the street, away from the waiting man and their home. Fires rage as the universe fills with light. The first stars burn bright and briefly. Dying, exploding, finding each other again. Forming greater balls of fire, heavier. Elements join in greater complexity. The suitor parks the vehicle. Opens the sunroof. They gaze at where the stars once were. Finding no fire in the heavens they kiss. His hand never leaves her thigh. On the porch stars explode into the waiting man's vision. The skies are ablaze with fire. Heavy elements form in the chaos of explosions. Beautiful jewels of color grow from the flames. Gold is forged in the heat, waiting to become a ring for her. Her hand finds that of the suitor and brings it to her breast. He touches the elements that make her up, also once forged in the stars. They delight in the blackness of deceit. Proximity sweetening the deception. Relative position rupturing time. Delicate hope breaking without the waiting man's awareness. He sits watching the birth of light flood the infant universe and sees her as its grand reason. From one cheap thrill to the next she misses this great luminous flood. The eyes of her suitor are glowing brighter in her mind. But in time she will forget his name.

The birth of the cosmos blinds the waiting man. He is not big enough to accept its stature. His mind is too small to capture its meaning. He has placed the meaning in her hands, the same that now stroke the suitor's leg, teasing to go further. The suitor swells, thanking the missing stars above him. Waves of light penetrate the waiting man. His tears are no filter for the infinite brightness. The beginning washes over him suggesting the ending. The cold dark end when all matter has separated forever. In these hours billions of years pass. The waiting grows tiresome. The light wanes then becomes bright again. Millions of stellar deaths before him. In the car the seats are leaned back. They lie next to each other, hands intertwined. He speaks of her beauty in the darkness, not knowing the color of her eyes. The darkness grows. The suitor's face is unimportant. He is a symbol for her. One that may be filled by any multitude. On the porch waiting, he cries for creation. For the lights that must dim in time. Their death a show that no one will witness.

In the darkness the suitor kisses her deeply. Reads from a script designed to impress budding females. She laps at the words as though they were written for her. The lights of creation separate. Time flows faster. The expansion grows faster. On the porch he moves his gaze from the past to the future. He sees that time is one place. The stars move. Space moves. The distances become unfathomably vast. Too much so for human contemplation. The fear caused by the great ignition, the wonderful spread of light, is worse now. The cosmos will swallow the light in time. It becomes a flicker again as the distance between photons expands. The suitor wants more. He says so. She feels at him, making sure he has swollen to bursting. Tells him it's time she left. She exits the vehicle into the night. On the porch the waiting man sees the stars extinguish and the cosmos return to blackness. The state is timeless, cold, thoughtless and dying

Publications

1. **The Names of My Children** – first appeared in Emanations: When a Planet Was a Planet, 2021 Ed. Carter Kaplan, International Authors

2. **The Day the Hooks Came** – first appeared in Simultaneous Times Podcast Ep.44, 2021, Space Cowboy Books

3. **Phrogger** – first appeared in The Mods, 2022, Ed. Eric Fomley, Shacklebound Books

4. **Over Night** – first appeared in Simultaneous Times Podcast Ep.01, 2018, Space Cowboy Books

5. **Come Back Earlier** – first appeared in Simultaneous Times Podcast Ep.24, 2020, Space Cowboy Books

6. **Due Date** – first appeared in Samjoko Magazine, Fall 2022, Ed. Todd Sullivan

7. **Western Expansion** – first appeared in Luna Arcana Issue #4, 2019, Ed. Rohini Walker

8. **Free Download** – first appeared in Crossing Over, 2015, Ed. Dorothy Davies, Horrified Press

9. **An Off the Record Letter to the People Watching Back Home** – first appeared in Howl Vol.25, 2022, Ed. Renee Gurley

10. **Blue Gemini One** – first appeared in Pablo Lennis #430, 2023, Ed. John Thiel

11. **Homo paniscus** – first appeared in Schlock! Webzine Vol. 6, Issue 28, 2014, Ed. Gavin Chappell

12. **Night/Day** – appearing for the first time

13. **Night Patrol** – appearing for the first time

14. **We Are Not Safe Here** (as Frank Slater) – first appeared in Simultaneous Times Podcast Ep.07, 2018, Space Cowboy Books

15. **The Escape** – first appeared in Simultaneous Times Podcast Ep.70, 2023, Space Cowboy Books

16. **Solvent** – first appeared in West Coast Weird #5, 2021, Ed. Shane Robinson, Seventh Station Publishing

17. **Electrosmooth** (as Frank Slater) – first appeared in Simultaneous Times Podcast Ep.25.5, 2020, Space Cowboy Books

18. **Fucking Like Animals** – first appeared in Simultaneous Times Vol.1, 2018, Space Cowboy Books

19. **Welcome Home** – appearing for the first time

20. **Disophonia** – first appeared in Starlite Pulp Review #3, 2023, Ed. Brian Townsley & Jake Naturman, Starlite Pulp

21. **Birth of Fire** – first appeared in Octo-Emanations, 2020 Ed. Carter Kaplan, International Authors

Milton Keynes UK
Ingram Content Group UK Ltd.
UKHW030650130824
446895UK00001B/10

9 798227 103475